HOLDING DOWN A BOSS

BY LATOYA NICOLE

DEDICATION

ON TODAY, MY BABY TURNS 11 YEARS OLD. FROM THE FIRST DAY I LAID EYES ON YOU, I KNEW YOU WERE GOING TO STEAL MY HEART. EVERYTHING I HAVE DONE WAS FOR YOU. ALL THESE BOOKS, ALL THE GRINDING, ALL THE STRUGGLES I HAVE OVERCOME WAS BECAUSE OF YOU. YOU'RE SUCH A JOY AND I'M GLAD AS FUCK GOD CHOSE ME TO BE YOUR MOM. I LOVE YOU WITH EVERYTHING IN ME AND I HOPE I SHOW YOU THAT EVERY DAY. MIRACLE MONÉT RILEY, COULD YOU BE THE MOST BEAUTIFUL GIRL IN THE WORLD. PLAIN TO SEE, YOU'RE THE REASON THAT GOD MADE A GIRL. HAPPY BDAY BOO.

AKNOWLEDGMENTS

THANK YOU TO EVERYONE WHO MAKES THIS POSSIBLE. I HAVE AN ENTIRE TEAM I CAN COUNT ON TO GET MY BOOKS RIGHT. BRITNEE (WHEW CHILE I BE NEEDING THOSE TEXTS AND WORDS OF ENCOURAGEMENT. THANK YOU FOR BEING YOU. TABITHA, TODDY, BRIA, AND SHATINA. JORDYN THANK YOU BOO ALWAYS. ASH MY COUSIN, LOVE YOU. YOU GUYS ARE ALWAYS THERE WHEN I CALL ON YOU NO MATTER THE HOUR. VANESSA I APPRECIATE YOU FROM THE BOTTOM OF MY HEART. THANK YOU TANESIA FOR EVERYTHING YOU DO. WE ALL MADE THIS BOOK POSSIBLE.

VALERIE, WHEW GIRL YOU ARE MY HEADACHE BUT I LOVE YOU TO PIECES. THANK YOU FOR EVERYTHING YOU DO. YO ASS WILL CALL AND CURSE ME OUT AT 3 IN THE MORNING LOL BUT I WOULDN'T CHANGE ANYTHING. I LOVE YOU FROM THE BOTTOM

OF MY HEART. JUST KNOW YOU MEAN A LOT TO ME MUFUCKA. BUT WE AIN'T ARGUING IN 2022. GET YO LIFE TOGETHER LOL.

THANK YOU MIESHA FOR LETTING ME DO YOU DIRTY LIKE THIS. LOL I LOVE YOU BOO

Danyelle Blakely 2018

They said no weapons formed against me shall prosper.

But these weapons forming and they beating my ass- author

unknown

"Take yall asses to bed right now. If I hear another word, I'm coming in there with my stick. I'm trying to get me some of this good pipe, and I don't want to hear no fucking kids laughing and talking." Our guardian Miesha yelled through the door. The eyes rolled on ten hungry kid's faces as we heard her door slam.

You hear the stories of group homes on tv and in books, but you never actually think you would ever see one in real life. Especially when you have two parents who loves you very much and your life appears to be perfect. My parents weren't on drugs, and they didn't leave me at a hospital. They were as perfect as you can get.

We had a house in the suburbs, with the picket fence. My father was a pediatrician, and my mother was a school teacher. Cliché, but as I said, the perfect family. I walked in the door from school to hugs, sandwiches cut into shapes, and genuine questions about my day. Me and mom would go outside to the yard and play on my swing that hung from our tree. Or, climb in my tree house and have dates until my father came home.

He would walk in the door and tickle me until I couldn't control my laughter. Everything was great, until I begged them to take me to the beach house for the fourth of July. We were in the car singing and laughing when a deer came out of nowhere. I woke up in the hospital an orphan. I'm assuming my parents left everything to my only surviving uncle because they thought he would do the right thing. As soon as the check cleared, he dumped my ass on the doors of the police station, and I've been in a group home the last nine years.

I'm sixteen now, and my life had dramatically changed. It was days we went to bed only having sleep for dinner and there was no love in these walls. Miesha didn't give a fuck about us, and the only thing she cared about was turning a trick to get money for herself. She yelled and beat us often, but what was the alternative? Even though this was rock bottom, it could be worse. It was a couple of kids that came here and told us stories about homes they left, and this was heaven compared to that.

"Danyelle, we about to sneak out and go find some food. You coming with us?" my friend Kema said to me while grabbing her hoodie. It was a cold April night, so looking at the holes in our clothes caused me to shake my head, but it was either be cold or hungry.

"Might as well. This bitch will let us starve. Did you see her eating steak earlier? She talked to me the entire time as she scoffed that shit down. I should have punched her ass in the face and took her food." Kema laughed, but I was dead serious.

"Yeah, you would have been full, but out on your ass before you could say pass the A.1. You see how that white only pie worked out for Claude. Now, bring yo dumb ass on. We can steal you a steak." Knowing she was right, I grabbed my raggedy ass hoodie and followed them out the window. Miesha would be busy for a while, so we had enough time to sneak back in without being noticed.

Four of us piled out the window as the others turned over praying we brought them something back. I wasn't giving them shit though. I took the risk, and they scary ass just wanted to lay on they ass, so they could starve for all I cared. We used our fare cards and hopped on the bus making our way to North Riverside. As soon as we got to Chilis, we jumped off and ran inside. We knew the bus schedule and one would be coming in approximately two minutes.

We had no time to waste. Looking around at the patrons and their food, I picked which table I wanted and walked over. Grabbing their plates, I started dumping it in my bag while laughing at the shocked looks on their faces. They had no idea what was going on, and by the time they realized what was happening, I was out the door. Everyone was behind me as we ran to the bus stop and jumped on the bus that had just pulled up. As soon as we got to the back, we all fell out laughing and immediately dug in.

"Oh my God; this is so good. I'm hungry, but I need to save some of this for tomorrow." I nodded at Kema as I licked my fingers and agreed. This was the first meal I had in three days, because Miesha hadn't had any company over. She kept walking her ass in our room and we didn't get a chance to sneak out. Knowing that could happen again at any time, I needed to save some.

"We should stop at the store and get some snacks too. I could use an ice cold Pepsi to wash this shit down," Jonathan said in between bites. The bus got to our stop, so we got off and went straight for the corner store. It was a group of guys standing out front gambling and I immediately became nervous. Standing right there in all his sexy glory was Tico. He was a neighborhood dope boy, and I was gone off his ass.

Tico was tall, thick, covered in tats, with a very light complected skin tone. His slanted gray eyes, full lips, and fully inked body turned me all the way on. He was talking shit with a toothpick hanging off his lips as he bent down and rolled the dice. Tico was always dressed in the latest fashion and today was no different. He had on a red and white letterman jacket, with a Gucci T shirt underneath and Red Gucci sneakers. He looked up at me and his gray eyes had me stuck.

"Judging by the look of your clothes, you ain't got the bread to cover if you make me crap, so move the fuck out the way." I opened my mouth to say something but closed it and walked off. Kema had an arm full of shit, so I walked over to her whispering in her ear.

"Can you please get me some stuff. I don't want Tico to see me shoplifting." Her ass laughed and nodded.

"You know our motto. If you don't get the shit yo self, you starve." I nodded and turned towards the door. "But, since you my bestest bitch, I got you. I'm not sure why you give a fuck what he thinks since he will never give your young ass the time of day. But hey, do yo thang."

"Don't forget I'm a broke ass bum. I know he will never look at me, but a girl can dream can't she?"

"A bitch can too, but that's all the fuck it is. A dream. Gone and get out of here. I'll meet you around the corner." Mouthing thank you, I walked out the store and stood off to the side watching Tico.

"Fuck you staring at? It's late as hell, take yo ass in the house," he said with his gray eyes staring into me. I know he probably didn't give a fuck, but the way he said that had me feeling like he cared about me.

"I'm going now, Tico. Maybe you should do the same." Him and his boys started laughing and I was trying to see what was funny.

"These my streets, Lil Mama. I don't have to do a mufucking thing." I shrugged my shoulders and tried to hide the fact I was just happy he was talking to me.

"Danyelle, come on. We have to go."

"Bye, Tico. Be safe out here." His ass nodded and kept playing dice. I walked off towards Kema with the biggest smile on my face.

"Bitch, if I get caught I'm beating your ass. For a fucking corner boy. Bring yo ass on." I laughed, but I didn't appreciate her talking about my nigga like that. In my mind, we was like Bonnie and Clyde on the come up.

"He's a corner boy for now, but you can tell he won't be for long. Tico been making a name for himself and he's going to be that nigga. Watch." She looked at me and scoffed.

"Even if he is, bitch he not gone be with you. This is not me trying to be mean, I just don't want you hurt friend. You see the type of girls he be with. Don't front yo move." I didn't say anything else as we climbed back into our window. Tico was going to be mine one day.

Mantico St. Lauren

Leaving out my two bedroom house, I jumped in my Hell Cat and drove towards the trap house I was a lieutenant over. I needed to make sure the money was good, and I always did that shit myself. I was anal when it came to my shit, and everyone knew it. I'm sure my bread was good because it never came up short. They knew better. I was only twenty one years old, but I had already made a name for myself out here.

I was a nigga with a plan, and this was always a part of it. I knew that a nine to five would never give me the type of bread I wanted, so I studied the dope boys on the corner. The first time I saw my Uncle Shemar walk in the house iced out in MCM from head to toe, I knew I wanted the lifestyle he lived. His ass was killed in a drive by, so I never looked at him as the blueprint. He just planted the seed.

Pulling up to the trap, I got out and headed inside. Everyone was at their posts doing what they were supposed to be doing and that was what I loved about my crew. We were all efficient because we all liked our shit to run smooth. No problems equaled more money for us.

"Hey nigga. Quit walking around smiling and grab this bag and get to counting. We trying to finish up early around here, so we can go play ball at the courts," my nigga Mink said as he tossed a bag at my feet.

"You know I'm going through my shit with ease. I'm a mathematician around this bitch."

"Aight mathematician. All I know is that shit better be right and not a dollar off or I'mma shoot yo ass in them big ass lips. I bet you be sucking pussy and the booty at the same time don't you?" I laughed but ignored his comment as I sat down at my station. If they were hooping, all the chicks was going to be out there even though it wasn't that hot out. Whenever we went to the courts, the bitches flocked. And wherever there was pussy, there was me.

Thirty minutes later, I was wrapping up and ready to go. Today was a good day and I knew my crew being on point was pushing me one more step up the ladder. I put everything away and grabbed my phone off the table. Mink and the rest of the crew was sitting around as if they was waiting on me to finish.

"Damn, it's about time. I thought yo dumb ass was back there jacking off or some shit. Come on before it starts getting cold out." Mink was right, Chicago weather would change on your ass in a minute.

"Bring yo crying ass on. I know this the only way you can get some pussy, so let's go."

"Yeah aight. Ask yo mama how I had her ass bent over screaming my name." I gave his ass a look and he laughed under his breath. I walked over to my Hell Cat and this nigga followed.

"Fuck you going? I ain't say yo hoe ass could ride with me."

"Shid, this the pussy magnet. Bitches ain't checking for a nigga in a Nissan Altima. If they see me in this, they automatically give me the pussy. By the time they figure out I got a Nissan, they be done already gave me the ass. They can't ungive the pussy my nigga." I laughed as we climbed inside. I

was able to splurge with my bread because it was just me.

Mink had four kids and his baby mamas was tearing a lining

out his ass.

We pulled up to the courts and everybody piled out

their cars. They ass started setting up for a game as I stood by

the bleachers. A nigga was too fly to be out here running up

and down the court. We weren't out there five minutes when

the lil niggas that wanted to be down, and the bitches started

piling in.

I checked out the crowds and I wasn't impressed. My

eyes landed on the lil chick Danyelle, and I shook my head as

she stared at me hopeful. I knew she wanted me, but I didn't

fuck young pussy. Even though she was broke as hell, she was

cute as fuck in a homely kind of way. Her big eyes looked at

me as if they were begging me to let her come over.

Her hair was pulled back into a ponytail that reached

her back. I knew it wasn't weave and that shit was rare in our

day and age. Her clothes fit her slightly overweight body

tight. You could tell they were handed down to her, and she was trying her best to fit inside them. Lil mama's round brown face was pretty as fuck though and she had the perfect smile hidden by pouty lips. Realizing I was staring at her ass, I turned my head to the game.

I was surprised Danyelle hadn't walked over to me yet, shorty always found a way to make conversation with me. Even though most mufuckas questioned why I entertained it, it didn't bother me. In this life, I knew it was rare finding genuine people out this bitch and I could tell she was real. Wasn't shit popping off, so I walked over to the nigga that came and set up a table. When the weather got warm, mufuckas in Chicago would set up a table and sell you just about anything off that mufucka.

"What you got today nigga?" I asked.

"Flamin hots or Doritos with cheese, and you can get meat on em too. I got some pops, and candy. What you want?" I saw Danyelle standing to the side out the corner of my eye and I laughed. Her ass looked nervous as fuck.

"Hey Lil Mama, you want something from over here?" She walked towards me slowly and looked over the stuff on the table.

"Can I get some Flaming hots and Doritos mixed with meat and cheese?" Her ass was shy, but not about food.

"Give me that too, with some sour cream and peppers. Oh, and two sodas. Nigga, fuck is you doing? Don't touch my shit bare, put some fucking gloves on before I beat yo ass."

"You got it." I turned towards Danyelle, and I could tell she was nervous as fuck.

"Why the fuck you not in school? You can't be no lil dumb bitch out here; that shit ain't cute."

"I didn't feel like it. I'm glad I didn't." She looked at me with a smile on her face and I shook my head. Our stuff was ready, so I reached out and grabbed it handing her a tray and a pop. Once I got mine, I walked off towards the bleachers.

"Hey, that's five dollars and fifty cents." The dude yelled at my back, and I threw up my middle finger. I looked back and Danyelle was following behind me like a lil puppy, but I didn't mind. It was boring as fuck out this bitch, and shorty was cool.

"Thank you for my food." I looked up to tell her she was good, when I noticed her shit was damn near gone.

"Damn, you good? Yo ass slamming that shit ain't you?" She gave a nervous laugh and I decided to let her make it.

"What's up Tico, you leaving with me?" This lil chick named Sheena I fuck with from time to time walked up and stood in front of Danyelle like she wasn't there.

"Don't you see me talking? Rude ass bitch. Get the fuck out my face while I'm eating and shit."

"Who you talking to, this fat ass homeless bitch? Boy bye. You trying to get this pussy or what?" Danyelle didn't respond, she just stood there looking like she was about to cry. I was about to drag Sheena's ass for questioning me when shots rang out.

Everyone was running, but I was trying to make sure Tico was good. I knew I should have gotten out the way, but I couldn't bring myself to leave not knowing if he was okay. I saw him across the court running towards the gates shooting at someone. Just seeing him fearless and busting that shit had me wanting him more. I could hear the sirens, so I threw reason to the wind and ran across the courts.

"Tico, come on we gotta go." His ass wasn't listening, but the police were close, and I didn't want his ass to go to jail. Grabbing his arm, I snatched him hard and pulled him until he voluntarily followed me. My house was across the street, so that's where I ran to. When I sat down on the porch, a bitch felt like I was about to die. I couldn't breathe and had to catch my breath.

"Hey Lil Mama, thank you for getting a nigga out of there." I nodded because I couldn't talk. When he realized a bitch was dying, he started laughing. I finally got my breathing under control and responded.

"You welcome. Yo dumb ass was about to get caught." He looked at me for a while with a weird look on his face making me feel self-conscience. "What?"

"Nothing, I appreciate that. My niggas ran away like some bitches, but you made sure a nigga was straight. You wasn't scared?"

"Hell naw. I've seen worse. I was pissed cus that rude ass bitch made me drop my food when she took off running. It was fye as fuck and now my ass gone be hungry." He really started laughing then and his smile was so fucking sexy.

"You said that like it was going to be your only meal for today. I ain't gone lie though, that shit was good." I looked across the street at the police walking around trying to talk to people to see what happened. I was trying to ignore his comment.

"You better give me your gun just in case." He looked at me weird, and then passed it to me. I tucked it away without a thought.

"Well, what the fuck do we have here? I know you ain't brought no nigga to my house? You don't pay no bills in this bitch, so you don't get no dick in this mufucka." Tico started laughing, but the sound of Miesha's voice irritated my soul.

"We were just talking." She walked down the stairs looking at the commotion and I couldn't do shit but laugh at her fake ass booty. It was one of them pads, but it still looked a mess. How you get a fake booty too small?

"Mmm hmmm. What the fuck going on over there? Just know, if a cop shows up at my door, I'm beating yo ass and you getting the fuck out my shit."

"Ma'am, Danyelle didn't do shit. We just rapping, you feel me?" I was shocked he remembered my name. I told him that shit like a year ago, and now my ass was blushing.

"I ain't no fucking ma'am. You know she a minor right? I can give you what she can't. You want to come inside and talk to a real woman?" I fought back vomit as she threw herself at him. I didn't know how he was going to respond, but Miesha always got the niggas she wanted.

"Bitch please. I heard that stale ass pussy crumbling when you walked past. Go sit yo old ass the fuck down somewhere or fix yo ass. It's twisted. Danyelle, I'm about to head out. Yo mama tripping like a mufucka. I'll holla at you later." I wanted to scream out she wasn't my mama, but I decided to leave it alone. Tico walked out the gate and disappeared. I wanted to beat Miesha's ass, but I sat there looking stupid.

"Let me find out you fucking or catch a nigga in my shit. I'mma beat yo ass and drag you back to the fucking courts. Dumb ass gone sit there and let him disrespect me. I should make yo ugly ass sleep on the porch." Miesha talked shit all the way in the house and then slammed the door. I was about to head inside, when Kema came out the door.

"What the fuck you do to her grouchy ass? She in there going off and slamming all kinds of shit over the house." I laughed hard as hell as I looked back at the door making sure she couldn't hear me.

"Tico treated her ass and she mad." Kema looked at me like I was crazy.

"Girl, are you high? You gotta be smoking if you think Tico was over here."

"Bitch, he was. We were at the courts, and he bought me some food. We were talking when the shots rang out and I made that nigga come with me cus his ass was about to go to jail. We were sitting out here talking when Miesha brought her nasty ass out here cock blocking." Kema looked shocked and excited at the same time.

"Aww bitch, you fucked up. As soon as you got him over here, you should have sucked his dick. Right here on the porch. Call that shit stair a la head." When she started doing the hand motion and pushing her tongue in her jaw, I fell out laughing.

"You know damn well I wasn't about to suck no dick. Everybody ain't gotta do that to get a nigga's attention." She looked at me like I was crazy.

"Well, how the fuck else you supposed to catch it? You a broke bitch living in a group home. You gotta show him your strengths. You know we gotta do extra to get these nigga's attention."

"Hell, I ain't never sucked a dick before. That definitely ain't my strength. He prolly would have shot my ass. I hope Miesha suck some dick tonight. I need to go get some food. My big ass hungry as hell." I thought about my flamin hots with cheese and got mad all over again.

"We got a lil shit left upstairs. Come on, let's go in the house it's getting cold out this bitch." We walked inside and went upstairs. As soon as I walked in the room, I knew some shit was off. Seeing our bags on the floor, I went off.

"Who the fuck ate our shit?" Kema grabbed the bags and saw that they were empty and walked over to Walter fat ass.

"Yo lips greasy as a mufucka. You ate our shit? I see your back spreading; looks like you stole a meal," Kema said as she grabbed him around his neck.

"I didn't eat anything. I swear." Looking over at Jeana with tears in my eyes, I ran over and hit her in the mouth. They was the only two up there, so one of they ass had to do it.

"You ate my shit?" I didn't give her a chance to respond, I just kept hitting her. If I couldn't do shit else, I could eat and I could fight.

"What the fuck are yall up here doing? I know yall not tearing my shit up." I stopped swinging and tried to explain but I was out of breath.

"This ugly bitch ate my shit." Miesha started laughing and crossed her arms.

"Naw, I threw it away. You bitches out here stealing and shit and I'm not having it. Let me find some more shit in here; I'm going to call the police myself. Now laugh at that since you found what that lil nigga said so funny." She walked off and I had tears in my eyes. We were about to starve if she didn't have a nigga come over tonight.

"You just had to piss the bitch off. Thanks a lot friend." Kema sat on her bed and turned away from me. I know she was mad, but this wasn't my fault. Not knowing what else to say, I laid down in the bed and closed my eyes. It was going to be a long day.

Mantico St. Lauren

I stormed in the trap house mad as fuck. These niggas were in here laughing and playing cards like ain't shit happened. Even Mink was sitting there chilling like they ass ain't leave me at the courts. I went to grab my gun, but I remembered Lil Mama had my shit. They finally looked up and saw me, and Mink had the nerve to start making jokes.

"Damn nigga, I thought they got yo slow ass. You ain't got them Meg knees huh." I looked at this mufucka like he was crazy.

"You niggas left me in a shoot out. What kind of clown ass shit is that?" I was pissed, but Mink was looking at me like I was crazy now.

"What the fuck was we supposed to do, eat the bullets? You wanna run towards death. You must be a superhero or something. Bullets bounce off yo goofass," Mink said as he dapped up Fil.

"On BD, this nigga something."

"Mufucka, you not even a BD. You sound bout dumb as hell. On God, you bitches scary as fuck. Why you carrying around guns if you not gone use them mufuckas?"

"Cus we live to fight another day fool." They all laughed at Fil and I took a seat, but this nigga Nab was laughing too hard for my liking.

"Hey Mink, let me see your burner." He looked at me funny but handed it to me. He should have known me by now and my temper didn't allow foul shit. I didn't even give a warning when I raised my gun and shot Nab between the eyes.

"Damn Tico, what the fuck? Fil said since it was his cousin, and he was the one that brought him in the crew.

"You feeling something? If not, call the clean up crew and continue playing yo lil game my nigga. Ain't no fucking crew without me. The next time yall see me up on a nigga, you better light that bitch up like bombs over Bagdad. I ain't allowing no scary niggas to get money in my crew. I'm the hand that feed you bitches, you better make sure that bitch stay good." No one else said anything, so I left it alone. Fil called the clean up crew as I looked at the table like didn't shit happen. They were playing spades, and I ain't have shit else going on.

"Where the liquor and the bitches at? Yall in here having a kick back with hard legs." Mink looked over at Fil and gave him a look. I guess he was trying to see if I was good because that nigga didn't do shit but crack jokes. I smirked letting him know I was good.

"I mean, who you wanted us to invite? That fat bitch you was cornered off with? Yall looked real cute and cozy," Mink said in a matter of fact tone.

"First off, shorty ain't fat. She thick as hell. In the right fit, you would be able to see her curves good. Second of all, I don't fuck young bitches." This nigga put his hand on his chest like he was clutching his pearls.

"Well, excuse me. Seems like I have offended thee. Is you cool?"

"You know me nigga. Shorty just cool, but she solid as fuck. Why you niggas was running like some lil bitches, shorty made sure I got out of there good and hid my burner."

"I would like to be the best man at your wedding." Now Fil was talking shit. It was good to know they weren't harboring any feelings about me killing Nab because they was my niggas and I would hate to push their thoughts back.

"Fuck yall. How about that." Standing up, I handed Mink his gun, and I left they ass in there playing cards. Jumping back in my car, I drove towards Portillos. Lil Mama was upset when her food got knocked over, and for some reason I got the feeling that was all she had to eat. Since I had to go back and get my burner, I decided to feed her. Pulling in the drive thru, I ordered us both an Italian beef, fries, a lemonade, and a cup of cheese. I didn't know if she liked this, but a hungry mufucka couldn't be choosy.

I got the food and drove towards her house. As soon as I pulled up, I parked and just looked at her house. I didn't want to encounter her ratchet ass mama again, so I opted out of knocking on the door. I wish my dumb ass had gotten her number before I walked off. Seeing a light on upstairs, I hoped it was Danyelle's room and not her mother's. Getting out, I looked around for a rock or something I could throw. Not seeing any, I did the next best thing.

"Hey yo Danyelle," I screamed towards the window. I saw a shadow, and then her head appeared outside.

"Shh, before you get me put out. Give me a second and I'll come out." Laughing, I shook my head and got back in my car. That was the reason my ass stayed the fuck away from young chicks. They had curfews and all kinds of shit. She appeared out of nowhere, opened my door, and climbed inside.

"Hey." Her voice was soft and innocent.

"Can you get away or you stuck for the night?" I wasn't trying to fuck or anything, but I didn't like sitting on the block. I was about to eat, and I wouldn't be paying attention. The last thing I needed was to get caught slipping.

"Probably not. Miesha don't have no dick lined up for tonight, so she fucks with us to pass the time." I raised my brow and looked at her confused.

"You call yo mama by her first name?" She shook her head and then let out a breath.

"She's not my mother. I live in a group home and she's my guardian. My parents are dead." The conversation got heavy quick as fuck, and I had no idea what to say.

"My bad. We can sit here for a minute if that's cool. I brought you some food." Reaching in the bag, I handed her the shit that was hers and pulled mine out to eat. Before I could say anything to her, she was tearing that mufucka up. I didn't say a word, I just started on mine.

"Thank you Tico. I know you didn't have to, but I appreciate it." I nodded and kept eating my food as I checked the mirrors occasionally. "Here, I'm guessing you might need this if someone runs up on you. I see you keep checking the mirrors." She handed me my gun and I laid it on my lap.

"Good looking." I saw her close her food up, but she wasn't done eating. "You don't have to stop eating on my account. I'm not one of those niggas. If you hungry, eat mufucka." The look she gave me told me that wasn't it. "I know you don't know me like that, but I'm a good ear. So, talk. What's yo story." She sighed, but I noticed she didn't open her food back up.

"It's some days we don't eat. If I eat it all now, I'll probably starve tomorrow. Most of the times I see you in front of the store, I'm in there to steal. Miesha don't give a fuck about us, but I'm not trying to go somewhere worse." I nodded in understanding, but I was at a loss for words.

"Eat Dany, I'll bring you something tomorrow." I have no idea why I felt bad for shorty, but normally I didn't give a fuck. She was nothing to me, so why should I care if she ate or not? That's how I would have looked at it had she not looked out for me. Slowly, she opened her bag and started eating. "Keep talking." I was trying to take away her feeling embarrassed, so I continued to eat as she told her story.

"My parents died in a car accident, and I ended up here. As long as I fend for myself, I'm okay most days. We be hungry as fuck in this bitch, but like I said, it could be worse." I looked at the holes in her clothes and wanted to tell her she was at worse, but I put a fry in mouth instead.

"Most people shit ain't perfect. My family did what they could, but I wanted more. Even though I'm good now, I still want more. This shit is going to be mine one day. Believe that shit. You just have to want more Lil Mama."

"I do want more for myself, but it's hard to get it with Miesha stopping me at every turn. I can't afford to get kicked out. I have no one." I didn't like emotional shit, so that was my cue to get the fuck on.

"You'll figure it out. I'll be by here tomorrow to bring you something to eat. Any requests?"

"I would love a good juicy fat ass burger." I looked at her and laughed.

"Aim higher Lil Mama. Your expectations low as fuck. If a mufucka telling you they will bring you anything in the world to eat, you don't ask for a burger. I'll pick yo meal. Now, get the fuck out my shit before ol girl come and put you out."

"Bye Tico." Lil Mama climbed out my whip and I fell the fuck out when I saw her climbing up the side railing and then through the window. Shaking my head, I pulled off once I saw she was inside safe.

I fell in my bed with the biggest smile on my face. I couldn't believe I was just with Tico. It was like we were on a date, and he actually gave a fuck about me. I knew that wasn't the case, but that's what it felt like. Even when I told him how fucked up my life was, he didn't look down on me.

"Girl, why the fuck you over there smiling like you just got some foot long dick?" Kema was staring at me waiting on me to give her the tea.

"I was just with Tico. He brought me some food." I realized my mistake the moment it left my mouth.

"Really bitch. I steal for yo ass out the store, but that nigga brings you some food and you couldn't bring me a bite knowing I was in this bitch starving. My stomach in my back, and you didn't think about me once." I could tell she was hurt, but that wasn't my intentions.

"I'm sorry Best. I closed the bag up to bring it inside, but he told me to eat it. When I told him how we don't eat most days, he made me finish it and promised to bring me more tomorrow." She had a look on her face that was a mixture of I'm happy for you and fuck you bitch.

"Awww Best. At least one of us got something. I'm not mad, just hungry. Just know, tomorrow we going stealing and everything yo ass get is going to be for me. You owe me hoe." I walked over to her bed and laid down beside her.

"Bitch, if you was mad it wouldn't have stopped my high. That nigga looked so good, I wanted to attempt to suck that thang."

"I'm gone have to teach you. Yo ass not about to be out here with the sexiest nigga in the hood embarrassing me. What else did he say? Yall gone get together or what?" I shrugged my shoulders.

"Bitch, nothing. He said I need to aim higher and that's what the fuck I'm gone do. It might not be today, but I promise I'mma get that nigga. Watch."

"The same way you aggressively said watch. You know how you tightened yo jaws and shit. Do the same thing when you sucking that dick; you gone get him." We both fell the fuck out laughing. Kema did too much and the shit she says out her mouth be having my ass in tears.

"Take yall dumb asses to sleep. If I have to come in there I'm beating ass and dragging you to the basement. Try me." We giggled, as I got out of her bed and climbed back into my own. Closing my eyes, I smiled until sleep found me.

****

Jumping up, I ran to the shower and got in before everyone else woke up and used all the hot water. I had no idea when Tico was coming, but I wanted to be ready. I washed my ass with a new purpose and the cheap ass dollar store soap Miesha bought us never felt better. I knew I was kind of on the big side, so I made sure my hygiene was always on point. Getting out, I made my way back to our room and looked through the few clothes I had. All my shit was fucked up, but I tried to find something without holes in it.

I know we stole food, but I wasn't trying to get caught in a store stealing clothes and shoes, and get my dumb ass locked up. I only had one shirt without holes in it, so I grabbed that and some jeans. Jonathan woke up and sat up on his bed as I stood to slide my panties on. After living in the same room for years, none of us was shy. When I finished, I went to the mirror and tried to comb my hair. It wasn't much I could do, since Miesha wouldn't buy us hair products, but I wanted my ponytail to be presentable.

"Girl, you in here acting like yo ass going to the prom. Do you even know what time he coming?" I rolled my eyes at Kema as I laughed.

"Hell naw, but I want to be ready. You need to quit talking so much shit, you coming across as a hater and that shit ain't cute."

"Neither is that dry ass ponytail. Come here. I stole some edge control, so let me at least swoop yo shit for you." Sitting on the bed, I sat there as she got the brush and the stuff for my edges.

"I don't want him screaming my name at the window, so will you sit on the porch with me?"

"Hell yeah. Just know I'mma get some of that food he brings you if I sit my ass out there." All I could do was laugh. It was a shame how our entire day consisted of finding something to eat. "You know if we would have gone to school, we could have at least had breakfast and lunch, right?" I thought about that, but I was scared to leave.

"Yeah, but what if he comes while I'm at school? I know my reason for not going, why the fuck yall still here?"

"Shid, this my Best first date. I wasn't missing that shit for nothing." Reaching up, I hugged her tight. We didn't have much, but we had each other. "Aight, enough of that. Let's go sit outside and wait for your man." We headed outside and sat on the porch. It was a nice day thankfully, so we won't be out here freezing our asses off.

At least that was what I thought, until we had been sitting in the same spot for eight hours. This nigga lied to me, and I was disappointed as hell. It was now cold as fuck outside, dark, and Miesha was gone start talking shit soon.

"Come on Best, he not coming." I could see the pity on her face, but I didn't want that shit. What I wanted was for her to say let's go beat that nigga's ass. "Maybe something happened." I nodded and stood up to walk inside. I was cold and I was tired of looking stupid. It was one thing to look dumb alone, but it was another having a witness to the shit.

Hearing an engine roaring down the street, I stopped in my tracks and looked. Tico pulled up and parked his car right in front of the house. I couldn't stop the smile that spread across my face.

"Bitch, have some dignity. Don't let his ass see you thirsty. Sit down and quit smiling." Doing as she said, I waited for him to come on the porch. When he walked up, it took everything in me not to smile again. He was wearing a Burberry cap, with a white tee, black letterman jacket, black jeans, and some Burberry sneakers. His ass always looked on point and I just wanted to be all in that nigga's skin.

"What up Dany. My bad for coming so late, it was some shit going on at the trap." I could see Kema damn near about to jump out her chair from excitement.

"Ain't yall cute. Mufuckas got pet names and shit. I'm her Best Kema, and no I'm not leaving. I want some of whatever is in that bag. So, hand it hea good sir." He laughed and passed her a bag.

"I was about to eat with Lil Mama, but you can have mine. Here Dany." He passed me a bag and I couldn't wait to see what was inside. When I pulled out the plastic bag, my eyes got big. Everyone was always talking about a seafood boil, but I had never had one. Not wasting any time, me and Kema dug in.

"What happened at the trap, is everything okay?" He looked shocked that I asked that but sat down on the step and faced me.

"Our shit always on point, but our money was off today. I thought I was gone have to kill one of my lil niggas, but our brick count was off. So, it's straight now. What you do today?" I didn't expect him to finish his story that fast, and my big ass had a crab leg in my mouth trying to crack it.

"Nothing, sat on the porch." He looked at me and then Kema.

"You been waiting on me all day?" When I nodded, I could tell he felt bad.

"Damn, I wasn't thinking. I'mma give you my number. Next time just call me and be like damn, bring my food." He laughed, but I started smiling.

"Next time?"

"You gotta eat right? If I don't bring it, you gone climb yo hungry ass out the window and go stealing. So, yeah, I got you. It ain't shit but food." It was just food to him, but it was everything to me.

"Ummm, not to interrupt yall lil fake date, but what about me? You either gotta buy enough for me, or let my Best bring me half of hers." Kema didn't have no shame in her begging.

"Damn Best, let a nigga offer your ass a meal. Begging ass. But I got you," he said like she was really his friend.

"What the fuck yall hot asses doing out here? Ohhh, this lil nigga back sniffing around. I guess he like funky pussy because you bitches smell bad. Get yall lil stanking asses in the house and throw that shit away." Ain't no way I was about to throw my food away. This shit was too good, and I still had some left.

"Miesha, can we please finish our food. We ain't ate nothing all day." She looked embarrassed and that was my point.

"Why yall didn't go in there and fix something? I ain't know yall haven't eaten. Gone head and finish. As soon as you done, bring yall asses in the house. Lil nigga, I'mma need you to get off my porch. My babies underage." Me and Kema looked at each other with our faces frowned up. She was putting on a world class performance.

"Calm all that loud shit down. We just cool and I'mma get up out of here after I make sure they eat." Miesha was pissed as she stormed in the house and slammed the door. Just as Tico said, he sat there until we were done.

"Aight Dany, I'm out. I'll be through here tomorrow."

"Bye Tico." When he drove off, I looked at Kema and stood up.

"You know she about to fuck us up right?"

"Yeah, I know," Kema said with fear in her voice. We opened the door and walked inside. As soon as we stepped all the way in, Miesha spoke to us calm as fuck.

"Go to the basement." We already knew what that meant, so the tears formed in my eyes. It was no way around it, so we both went down the stairs.

"You think the food was worth it?" Kema looked at me and we both answered my question at the same time.

"Fuck yeah."

Mantico St. Lauren

Walking into Manny's office, I tried to catch my breath. It wasn't a good look going to see the boss looking weak and shit, but his house was big as a mufucka. It had to be at least two blocks long and a nigga was tired as shit. It wasn't often I got called in, because I kept my crew in check and things went smooth. If Manny called you to his house, that meant something was wrong. I wasn't nervous, but I was ready for anything at this point.

"Have a seat." Doing as I was told; I crossed my hands over my stomach and waited to see what was up. I wasn't about to try and figure it out because I knew I had done nothing wrong. If he had an issue that was on him, and he was gone have to state that shit. He stared me in the eyes as if he was waiting on me to break, but he had a better chance of Oprah looking like Halle Berry.

Some naked bitch walked in during our stare down with a bottle of Scotch and poured him a glass. When she walked over to me, I put my hand up to stop her. I needed to be alert just in case I had to kill this bitch ass nigga. He took a sip of his drink, then placed the cup down all while never taking his eyes off me.

"You know in this life; you have to have an exit strategy. It's no forever in this shit, and you have to keep that in mind, or you will get stuck in this shit. Don't wait until shit is going bad because that usually means it's too late. The time to walk away is when that money is right, and everything is going good. You had a great run and it's time to pass the torch." I knew he was dropping jewels, so I hung on every word he said, but I was trying to figure out where the fuck this shit was coming from.

"Makes sense-..." He threw his hand up to stop me from talking.

"I've watched you get this shit out the mud and your grind match mine. I'm going to be stepping down in about a year and I think you're ready." My palms started sweating from excitement, but I didn't interrupt him again. "If you're going to take over; I need you to stay away from the dumb shit. That shoot out at the courts the other day was dumb and reckless. It can't happen again are we clear?"

"Say less."

"You're a St. Lauren; act like it." I was about to stand up and leave, but something about the way he said that had me stuck.

"What that mean?" I always wondered who I was named after because my mother's last name is Gregory. She always said my father passed away, but it was never any other family. The way he said that shit had me feeling like he knew him.

"I wanted Yvette here when I told you this, but she refused to come today. The life I lived was reckless and dangerous. A lot of people were after me and it wasn't safe to raise a family. I asked Yvette to have an abortion, but you know your mother. Even though I wasn't trying to put yall in danger, I wanted to do the right thing, but your mother wanted out. She didn't want you growing up in that lifestyle, she always said she wanted you to be better than me.

When you started running the streets anyway, Yvette came to me and asked me to look after you. It was something she couldn't stop, but Yvette wanted you protected. I appreciated how you turned my first offer down and opted to grind your way to the top. I've kept eyes on you at all times and you're a natural at this shit. I've had a good run and I'm ready to leave all this shit to you." I took in everything he said, and I was pissed.

"Nigga, we struggled and you was out here living like this because my moms said she didn't want me in your lifestyle. Nigga I'm your blood, so I'm already in it." He nodded, but I could tell he was hot. His jaw line was jumping, but I didn't give a fuck.

"Your mother is a millionaire. I'm not some lame ass nigga that don't do for his kids. We did what we thought was right, even if it wasn't. Whatever the case may be, you watch your tone when talking to me." His anger wasn't moving me.

A mufucka just sidetracked me with some shit and think I was supposed to be happy about it.

"It seems like you and moms got it all figured out. Fuck you need me for?" Every vein in his body was popping out by this point, but I never changed my tone. Fuck him.

"I need you to take over the business. It's your birth right and you earned it."

"I need time to think." Leaving out, I headed towards my car with a lot on my mind. I never knew my moms was capable of holding secrets from me and that shit had me bugging. Looking at my watch, I saw it was now three. I didn't want Dany and her homie waiting on me again, so I decided to take them some food before I went to holla at my moms. I really wasn't in the mood for all that shit, but a nigga gave his word. I knew if I handled my business first, I would be leaving her hungry. In my line of work, shit could come up and I couldn't be tied down to that shit every day. Thinking of another way, I drove towards the grocery store.

Parking, I got out the car and walked inside. A nigga didn't know what all you needed to cook, but it was gone have to do. Grabbing a bunch of steaks, packs of chicken, ground beef, and any kind of meat I could find; I threw it in the buggie. After getting sides, pops, and other bullshit I thought they might like, I was heading towards their house. Just as I thought, they were sitting on the porch when I pulled up. Waving Dany over, I watched as she nervously walked to my car.

"Hey Tico. You not sitting with us today?" I could see she wanted to be under me, but I wasn't with that shit either. Shorty was cool and I appreciated the fact she was solid, but I don't sit on porches and shit shooting the breeze.

"Naw, I got some shit to handle. I need you and ol girl to do me a favor though. I forgot to get you some snacks. Go run around the corner to the store for me." Reaching in my pocket, I gave her a twenty and she walked off towards the porch. I waited until her and her friend was out of sight before I grabbed the groceries out my car. Walking to her door, I knocked.

"I knew yo fine ass was going to come back for this pussy. You just in time too, them bitches just left." Pushing my way inside, I walked around until I found the kitchen and dropped the bags. "Damn baby, you want me to cook for you first?" Turning around, I grabbed her by her throat and slammed her through the table.

"You took these fucking kids in. Nobody made you do that shit. You did it because you portrayed yourself to be a good person. I brought you groceries and shit for you to cook for them. If I find out they ain't been eating or you beating on them, I'm coming back. Trust me, you don't want me to come back. Do you want me to come back Miesha?"

"No. I don't." Grabbing her by her hair, I snatched her up off the floor.

"Cook them something good too. Stupid ass bitch. Oh, and Miesha, you left yo ass on the floor." She looked down and noticed her booty pad had slid from under her dress.

Shaking my head, I walked out and went back to my car. It was perfect timing since I saw Dany rounding the corner. They crossed the street and came over to my car.

"We got the snacks. Thank you Tico." I could tell she was waiting on the food.

"Aight. I'll be around to check on you. Yall be good out here. Miesha in the house cooking for yall." Confused looks crossed their faces, but I had to go. I didn't have time to do all that explaining shit.

"So, you not coming over anymore?" Dany eyes looked sad, and it almost had a nigga feeling like shit, but I had more important shit going on. I would check in from time to time to make sure Miesha kept her word, but other than that I had moves to make. Yeah, I was pissed at my moms and Manny for keeping secrets from me, but I would be a fool to turn down the empire.

"I said I'll check in from time to time. Yall be good out here." Not waiting on her to keep looking at me like I was the bad guy, I pulled off. I had other shit to do. First thing was going to holla at moms.

Danyelle Blakely

It's been months since I last saw Tico and I was in my bag about that shit. I don't know what he said to Miesha, but she been cooking for us every day. Her ass was being so nice, we were almost scared to eat it. Shit been weird around the house now that she wasn't fucking us up, but I hated not seeing Tico. He didn't even keep his word about checking on us, and it was really looking like fuck him right now.

"How the fuck you just gone come in here and steal my pussy? You got me fucked up nigga." Me and Kema looked at each other and fell out laughing. Miesha was arguing with her latest fuck and the shit was funny as hell. We eased closer to the door to hear her more clearly.

"You thought that weak ass pussy and fake ass was worth my bread? You got me fucked up. Plus, I ain't steal shit. You gave it to me," the dude she was with said pissed off.

"Nigga, if you fuck me and don't pay, yo ass stole it. Get yo weak ass and your weak ass stroke the fuck out of my house." Moments later we heard the door slam. That bitch acted as if her pussy was sculpted by God himself. She oughta be shamed out here charging niggas for basic pussy.

"One of yall bring yall asses down here and clean up my fucking kitchen. This shit better be done in twenty minutes or I'm dragging yall bitch asses to the basement." Rolling my eyes, I went out the door to get it done. If we sat around trying to figure out who was gone do it, shit was only going to be bad for all of us.

"I'll help you Best." Me and Kema went in the kitchen and started washing the dishes and putting everything away.

"It would be your fat ass to come down here. Don't you think I'm tired of seeing your fucking face? You think you big shit huh since you got that boy sniffing around here looking after you. Bitch, you just big and I'm not scared of that nigga." I bit my jaw and tried my best to ignore Miesha, but you could tell she was determined to take it there. "Oh, now your bitch ass can't hear. Go to the basement, both of you bitches."

"Mie, we didn't even do nothing. You asked us to clean up and that's what we doing. So, you telling me we about to get fucked up because we did what you asked?" Kema asked in a confused tone. Out of nowhere, Miesha threw a plate at her, and blood immediately poured from her forehead.

"I don't give a fuck. I said go to the basement." We both headed downstairs, and the tears began to fall. Accustomed to the abuse, we kneeled down in front of the sink waiting for her to come fill it up. I had no idea what kind of sick mufucka would think of something like this, but we were used to it. Miesha walked behind us filling the sink up with water. As soon as it was to the rim, we stood up as she pushed our heads inside. We immediately began gasping for air. This was the first time she held us down there this long, usually, she brought us back up after about ten seconds. I was feeling faint and ready to pass out because it's been about thirty this time. Finally, right when it felt like I wasn't gone make it, she pulled us up.

Me and Kema started choking spitting up water trying to catch our breath. She didn't give us time to recuperate when she grabbed a pole and started beating us with it. My big ass tried to duck under the sink but ended up positioning myself for the pole to hit me in the eye. I knew that bitch was gone be black, but I couldn't worry about that right now. A bitch was trying to stay alive. Thankfully, she got tired and walked off without saying another word.

"Best, we gotta get out of here. I think this bitch really tried to kill us this time." I looked at Kema still choking while trying to get off the floor.

"Where we gone go? We only have a couple more years and we will be out of the system. We just gotta hang in there and stay out of her way."

"We didn't do anything wrong tonight. Hell, we never do, and she still fucked us up. It has to be better for us out there somewhere." We both started crying as we made our way up the stairs.

"Best, you remember the house you came from? There is no better. We just gotta stick it out." She reached up and wiped the tears from my eyes and then looked at me.

"I thought it was gone wipe off, but it didn't. She fucked you up and you really out here ugly as shit right now." We both started laughing as we made our way to our room. I couldn't help but think about Tico. What was so important that he stopped checking on us? Whatever he said to her that day had her shook, and she was being nice. I'm guessing since she hasn't seen him around she figured he didn't give a fuck. I know I should be like fuck Tico, but I drifted off to sleep hoping he was okay.

****

"Get yall asses up. You think you gone lay around here all day and ain't gotta go to school. Get yall dirty asses the fuck out of my house and go to school now." Miesha was in the doorway screaming as we groaned and started getting out of the bed. My entire body was hurting like a mufucka, so I limped towards the door instead of walking regular. She looked at me and shook her head. "You can't even get your ass whooped right. Yo think you slick huh? Letting your eye get black, so them people can come around here asking me all types of questions. You not going no fucking where." I wanted to laugh in her face, but I didn't want to end up back in the basement.

How did I want to get my eye black? Bitch, you hit me in my shit. Fuck you mean. She sounded real dumb right about now, but I was grateful I didn't have to go to school. I prayed Miesha still let me eat, or that would be the only fucked up thing. I would be missing a meal. Kema walked over to me and kissed me on my jaw.

"I'll be back before you know it Best. Stay away from her as much as you can. I don't care if you have to hide in a closet. Don't go around her ass today." I nodded and she walked out the room.

I thought about how Tico came into my life momentarily and made my shit better. Then left us to fend for ourselves. I know we weren't his responsibility, but why start the shit if you wasn't gone finish it? I should have known that was too much to ask of a street nigga, but to me he was different. Always has been. From the first time I laid eyes on him, he stood out from the rest. He was a young nigga with hella swag.

I had only been here a couple of days, and I was sitting on the porch crying thinking about my parents. Him and his friends were standing across the street talking shit when some guy walked up acting tough. Everyone else was scared because he was so big, but not Tico. He hit his ass hard and fast. That big nigga dropped like the hoe he was, and I was shocked. Tico wasn't thick and tall like he is now. I couldn't believe someone so small had that much power in him. I should have known then I loved bad boys. I went from crying about my parents, to going outside hoping to see Tico every day.

For years, he is what got me through. Seeing him always brightened my day even if he was talking shit or ignoring me. I fell in love with his ass that day, but I know it will never happen.

The nigga couldn't even keep his word, so I don't know why I'm tripping off him. Closing my good eye, I pictured his ice gray eyes and I couldn't stop the smile that spread across my face. I had it bad, and I had no idea how to shake that shit.

Mantico St. Lauren

"Fuck, yo head fye as fuck. Deep throat my shit." This girl named Tyra was topping me off in my car and a nigga toes was curling in my gym shoes. Shorty was only eighteen, but gave head like a pro. That only let me know she sucked a lot of dicks out here, so I couldn't cuff her, but I made sure she hit me off from time to time.

"Mmmm, this dick so fucking big," she said as she deep throated my shit with no gagging. If I wasn't confident, shorty would have had me feeling like I had some lil meat. Grabbing her by her head, I continued to push her head down knowing she couldn't go any further.

"Damn girl. Spit on it." Tyra did as she was told, and she had my ass going in this bitch.

"I wanna ride it." I really wasn't in the mood to be trying to fuck in the car, but I needed to get this nut off. Grabbing a condom, I slid it on my dick and moved my seat back. Shorty climbed over fast as fuck sliding down on it. Out of nowhere, she started bucking hard as fuck.

"Hey, slow the fuck down before you break my shit and I beat yo ass." She started giggling, but I didn't find shit funny. Mufucka was throwing ass sweat all over my car and bumping against my steering wheel. I didn't play about my shit. Now, I had an attitude, and I needed this shit to be over with. Gripping her ass, I slammed her up and down on my dick trying to rush my nut. Once I got mad, everything irritated me about a person. I guess it was the Cancer in me, but I was annoyed at the way the bitch moaned now. Her voice had my dick going soft.

"What's wrong?"

"Nothing. I just need you to shut the fuck up and ride this mufucka."

"Okay daddy, I got you." And just like that, my shit was soft as noodles.

"Man, get the fuck up. Yo ass don't listen. I'll holla at you another time, I gotta go make some moves." She had an attitude out of this world as she fixed her clothes.

"Can I at least get some money this time?" Now, that had me laughing hard as fuck.

"How many times I gotta tell you? I don't pay for pussy shorty. Wrong nigga." I looked at her letting her know I was waiting on her to get out my shit. Every time we fucked, she asked the same damn question, and that shit worked my nerves. If it wasn't for the head shot, I would have been stopped fucking with her ass. Tyra climbed out slamming my door in the process. Shaking my head, I tossed the condom out the window and fixed my clothes.

"I'm glad you over here happy and shit. Meanwhile, we over there getting our ass beat and starving." I looked up and saw Dany's friend in my window.

"Fuck you talking bout?"

"You told Dany you would come around and check on her. Since you haven't, Miesha been taking her anger out on her because of you. I know you called yourself helping, but you could have kept that shit if you wasn't gone stand on what you said." Even though I was pissed at this lil girl telling me what the fuck I should or shouldn't be doing, I was irritated that Miesha didn't heed my warning. Anybody I encountered knew once I said something, that shit was law. I see Miesha thought this shit was a game and I was gone have to show her dumb ass who the fuck I was.

"Get in." Shorty got in the car with her nose turned up and I couldn't do shit but laugh.

"Ewww, you just in here fucking bitches with funky pussy. You got too much money for that."

"Man, shut the fuck up. You young bitches today talk too damn much. How you gone get a ride in my shit and then talk smack?"

"Well, I didn't ask to get in this funky mufucka. I just saw your shit parked and decided to tell you bout yo self. I had to wait two minutes for you to finish. It wasn't long, so that was cool." I could hear the shade in her tone and laughed as I drove off.

"Bruh, you talk too much. Stay in a child's place. You don't know shit about how long I take."

"Mmm hmmm. Like I said, I was there for the whole two minutes. It's cool though. If she like it, I love it. I'mma have to tell my Best don't waste her time though."

"Naw, you gone mind yo business." I don't know why it bothered me that she was going to tell her that, but it did. Shorty was too young for me, and we didn't fuck around, so I shouldn't have cared what the fuck she knew. I pulled up to the house and parked my car. "Take this bread and get Dany. I need yall to go to the store." She smiled as she took the money and jumped out. Grabbing my burner, I closed my eyes and thought about what I was going to do. I had a strict code. No women and no kids, but this bitch was trying me.

I also told Manny I would move smarter, since I was now being groomed to take over. I looked over and Dany was coming out the house. We locked eyes and I could see the disappointment on her face. Not wanting to admit I played them dirty by staying away, I turned my head. What the fuck did they want from a nigga? I wasn't her man, and I had no ties to them. I called myself helping out and done bit off more than I could chew. Taking a deep breath, I got out the car and headed towards the house the minute they were out of view.

Walking inside, I looked around but didn't see Miesha. Looking in all the rooms, I found her inside of one sleeping peacefully like death wasn't knocking at her door. Going over to the bed, I sat down but she didn't move. Using my gun, I tapped her against her forehead. When she still didn't move, I hit her hard in the head.

"What the fuck is going on?" She jumped up looking confused.

"The last time I was here, I know I said I didn't want to come back. I also made sure that you were clear. Yet here I am." Putting the gun to her temple, I allowed my words to sink in.

"I.. I'm sorry. I was having a bad night."

"Naw, see I'm not really buying that shit. When someone fears someone, it doesn't matter what they got going on. They will cross they mama before they cross you. Me not coming around had you feeling like you could do what you want, and I have a problem with that." She tried to get loud with her pleas, but I wasn't in the mood for that.

"It won't happen again. I promise. Please, don't kill me." Knowing it's things I could do worse than death, I decided to go with that. Step one, taking away the one thing she thought was her selling point. Placing my gun against her fake ass, I pulled the trigger. I knew my shit was strong enough and was definitely going to pierce through. "Fuckkkkk. Oh my God. I'm so sorry. I won't do it again." Not knowing which hand she struck them with, I grabbed one and put a bullet through that mufucka as well. By this time, she was screaming and crying at the same time.

"Every time I have to come back, I will take a piece of you until there is nothing left. Are we clear?"

"Yes, Oh God yes. We're clear. It won't happen again."

"Go to the ER and get cleaned up. I'll have them fed tonight, but on tomorrow you better have your bitch ass walking around here singing and cleaning." I watched her limp out crying and I went to the porch waiting for Dany.

"What you think he did to her?" Kema was looking at me as if I was supposed to know. I really didn't know what Tico was capable of, but I hoped he killed her ass. She didn't deserve to raise another kid, with how fucked up she was.

"Ion know Best, but I hope it works this time if he didn't kill her."

"If she dead, where we gone live? They gone split us up and we gone have to go somewhere that's probably worse." That reality slapped us in the face often. Walking up to the porch, I was shocked to see Tico still here and sitting outside. Not really having anything to say to him, I let Kema give him his stuff and I walked inside. Going up to my room, I laid on my bed. Yeah, I wanted him, but he didn't get to treat me like I was shit. I can take that from everybody else, but not him.

Tico has always been my rainbow at the end of a storm. If I was having a bad day and I saw him, everything seemed better. I put him on a pedestal and that mufucka was falling. I get why people say if you don't put people up that high, they won't have that far to fall. Wiping a tear from my eye, I turned over on my side and attempted to go to sleep. Feeling my bed dip down, I knew Best had climbed in with me.

"You don't have to talk shit Best. I know he's not mine, but I expected more from him you know? He gave his word and then said fuck us. I don't know why I believed his ass in the first place."

"Because people make mistakes. Even me." Hearing his voice, I jumped up and turned around fast as hell.

"Tico, what are you doing up here?" Reaching out, he wiped the tear that was on my cheek and gave a weak smile.

"Because a nigga gave his word and I had to make sure you was good. I had a lot going on, but I'm here now, Lil Mama. I know my word don't mean shit right now, but I'mma make it up to you. I can't promise that I won't fuck up along the way, but a nigga gone try."

"Why?" He looked at me confused.

"Why what?"

"Why are you giving your word to help us? You don't like me and I'm nothing to you, so why are you doing all this?" He thought it over before answering.

"Do the why matter? If I told you it was no big reason behind this shit and it was just my good deed; doesn't it still get done? You're looking for some Cinderella type reason and this ain't that. If I said hey, I'm looking out for you because you did a solid for me, is that not enough? Quit looking for some fairytale bullshit to hold on to and just appreciate the fact that I'm here." It was hard to hear, but it was the truth. I guess I was looking for him to say cus I like you a little or for him to say I mean something to him. But, like he said; this wasn't that. I mean, but I wasn't some soft ass bitch, so I wasn't about to respond like one.

"On God, I'll take yo dick and make you my man. I'll make my own fucking fairytale." His ass looked at me and laughed hard as hell.

"Stop playing with me before I beat yo ass Dany. Come take a ride with me; I gotta get yall some food to eat tonight."

He stood up, so I did the same. "I'mma have to get yo ass some boxing lessons or something. You let that old ass bitch beat yo ass like that. In here ugly as a mutha fucka." My mouth opened and closed back. A bitch had to gather her thoughts hearing him say that to me.

"I know how to fight Tico. If I fuck Miesha up, then what? Can I come live with you?" I was nervous as hell waiting on his response.

"Learn how to duck then. I can't hang around a scary, ugly mufucka." Shaking my head, we walked downstairs together.

"Awww man Best. I forgot to tell you he was a two minute nigga. You disappointed? I can't tell cus your eye leaning and shit." I laughed at Kema because she was really moving in close trying to figure out my expression.

"I told yo lil young ass to find you somebody to play with. Now you gone starve tonight. I'mma teach yo smart mouth ass a lesson." I could see the hurt on Kema face, but I would give her mine before I let her starve.

"I was just joking. Please, don't do this to me." Tico looked like her begging fucked him up.

"I see you can dish a joke but can't take it. I'm not gone starve you, but you only get one wing and two fries. If I see you grab anymore, I'mma break yo fingers." She mushed him in the head, and his eyes turned cold.

"I don't play like that. If you ever put yo hands on me, you gone see another side of me." This was the first time I've seen Kema shut up. Normally, she has a snappy comeback, but she looked shook.

"I'm sorry." Tico didn't respond, he just walked out the door. I followed behind him, but now my ass was nervous. I climbed in his car and was damn near sitting on the door. His expression still hadn't softened, and I didn't know what to say.

"You good with Uncle Remus?" I've seen people get that chicken before, but I've never had it. The sauce on that shit be looking so good.

"Oh God, yes." He turned towards me and laughed.

"I see yo thick ass likes food. Besides eating, what you like to do?" He was waiting on an answer, but I was still beaming over the fact he called me thick. I started sticking my thigh out a lil bit trying to entice him. He noticed what I was doing and shook his head. Leaning over, he got really close to my ear and I swear I felt just like that bitch on the five heartbeats swarming in my seat.

"Is there a heart in the house tonight?" I didn't mean to scream that out, but a bitch was nervous as fuck.

"I'm telling you. That lil pussy not ready for a nigga like me. Quit dreaming about something that will fuck yo life up." He leaned back to his side of the car, but I was still stuck looking like a gang banging cricket. "Now, again. What do you like to do?"

"I don't know. I haven't done anything since my parents died. I used to go out back and play with my mom. We cooked together, but hell, that's still food. The only other thing I do besides surviving, is go to the courts to see you." He nodded, but I could tell that wasn't the answer he was looking for.

"So, you ain't gone have shit going on 'IF' you graduate from high school? How the fuck you expect to get away from Miesha if you have no life plans? You gotta have something going for you Lil Mama or you gone live a long hard life. All you gone end up doing is latching on to a nigga that treats you the exact same way she did. It's going to be what you're used to and all you know. Shid, it's going to be all you're worth. I told you aim higher, so the next time I see you I want you to tell me what you want to do with your life." No one has ever talked to me in that way and the shit had me stuck. When I saw Tico, I always looked at him as some fine ass nigga that was getting money. I could see he was more than that and it's sad to say, it only made me want to fuck him more.

"I don't think about my future. All I'm trying to do is survive around this mufucka."

"You are what you think Lil Mama. If you think you not gone be shit, then yo ass gone be exactly that. One thing I've learned in life is if someone tells you they getting what they deserve, let them get that shit. No one else can make you want better. Holla at me when you ready to elevate." I nodded, but I didn't know what he wanted me to say.

Mantico St. Lauren

Shit been going well on my streets, and I was satisfied with how everything was running smooth. I had my first meeting with my connect and I knew I wouldn't have any problems. This whole month, Manny been setting me up for the takeover. Normally when he dropped jewels, I soaked all that shit in because I knew he had the blueprint. Now, shit seemed weird since I knew he was my pops.

We been butting heads, but since I did my job well, it wasn't shit he could do but respect it. I didn't have to take life lessons from his ass, but he always seemed to throw them bitches my way. I was trying to adjust to the news, but this nigga was acting as if his ass been in my life. Getting out my car, I grabbed my keys, so I could run in my moms house. I smelled food cooking as soon as I stepped inside, so I headed towards the kitchen. She wasn't in there, so I washed my hands and immediately started looking in the pots.

"I hope yo raggedy ass washed yo hands."

"Gone head on with that bullshit. You know I'm not a nasty nigga. Don't play with me like that," I said as I pulled some of the pot roast out of the pan. I dropped the shit when she popped me in the back of my head.

"I know you think you the nigga out there in them streets, but in here I'm that bitch. Don't talk to me like I'm some hood rat. Now, again. Did you wash yo hands?"

"Yeah, ma. Damn." This time, I moved out the way before her hit could connect.

"Sit down. I'll make you a plate." As soon as my ass hit the cushion, she started in. "So, how are things going with you and your father?"

"I mean, ain't much changed except now I know why he be trying to give me advice. We mostly been talking about the business and shit though. He asks about you a lot. Have you talked to him?" She scoffed and placed my plate on the table.

"I only deal with you because you my child. I don't deal with that street life anymore son. I'm good on all that."

"You do know he's retiring right? So, if you don't want that street life then you good. Yall can be two old niggas laid up living a boring ass life." Grabbing my fork, I dug into my macaroni. I damn near moaned like a bitch this shit was so fucking good.

"He saying that, but you know how that goes. Niggas always talk about walking away, but they never do. You gone be one of them niggas too." That caused me to stop eating and think about what she said. If this nigga didn't walk away, it didn't come to me. That shit couldn't happen, this city was going to be mine no matter what.

"Naw, he retiring. His ass don't have a choice. Not for nothing, it's something I been wanting to ask you. Manny said you were a millionaire and he never left you to struggle. Is that true?" Her ass started fidgeting around, so I knew it was true.

"Does it matter?"

"Yeah, it matters. Hell, half the reason I was impressed by the street life was because I loved the glitz and glam. If I knew we wasn't broke, I prolly would have set my ass down somewhere." I could tell that pissed her off.

"Don't blame the shit you do on me. I didn't want any parts of that life and I didn't want you thinking that shit can be handed to you and life was easy. I thought you was going to see that your mother worked hard, so you should too. Instead, you took your raggedy ass out there and got in the streets anyway. We were always good, but you wanted to ball out of control. That wasn't me." I nodded in understanding and ate some cornbread.

"I feel that. You did good ma. I was just wondering what made you go to work every day and you had bread, but I get it. This food fye as fuck too."

"I know. Now, when you done clean your plate and lock up. I have a hair appointment."

"Say less." She walked out and I continued to eat my food. She had me thinking about the shit she said. Manny better not try that bullshit, or I was going to retire his ass one way or another. It was my time to shine, and I wasn't gone let him or no one else get in the way of that.

As soon as I was done, I cleaned up like she asked and thought about Dany. I hadn't been by to check on her in a week, so I needed to stop over there. Shit had been going good, but I can tell Miesha was one of them bitches you had to keep your foot on her neck. Grabbing some containers, I decided to pack Dany and her friend some food up. This shit was so good, someone else needed to taste it. My moms lived here alone, so her ass wasn't gone eat it all.

Leaving out, I locked up and jumped in my car. It didn't take me long to pull up at Dany's spot since she didn't stay far from my mom's house. Getting out, I walked on the porch and knocked on the door. I could see they were packed at the courts, so I will stop over there when I'm done. It took a minute, but Kema finally came to the door.

"Hey Tico. She not here, she over there looking for your raggedy ass. Oooh, what's in the bowls? I hope you brought some for me." I swear this girl didn't give a fuck about begging.

"Here, make sure you save Dany some. I'm about to go over there and holla at her. Shit been good here though, right?" Kema ass was closing the door on a nigga ready to go tear into the food.

"Everything is fine. Bye, brother in law. Thanks again for the food." I couldn't even correct her as she closed the door. Laughing, I ran down the stairs and across the street. It was a lot of people out here, so I was trying to find Dany. When I spotted her, I headed towards her, and her face lit up as soon as she saw me.

"Hey, Tico. You playing today or you just checking out the crowd?"

"Naw Lil Mama, I was looking for you. I stopped at your spot first and took you some food. I know yall been good, but my mama threw down and I wanted you to taste it." She started smiling when some clown ass nigga bumped into me. "Hey nigga, watch where the fuck you going." This mufucka looked at me like I was small.

"You better get yo goofass on. It's crowded, and you blocking the walkway like you own this bitch." My jawline started jumping and I could feel Dany's nervousness. Her ass started shifting from foot to foot.

"These are my fucking streets. You better ask some fucking body out here before you lose your life. Now get yo dumb ass the fuck on." This lil nigga started laughing and walked in my face like I was a bitch. I heard Manny's voice in my head, and I knew I couldn't kill this lil nigga in broad daylight with all these witnesses, but he was pushing me.

"Do something then, bitch." Since I couldn't kill his ass, I decided to teach him a lesson. Grabbing my burner, I shot his ass in both legs. One thing I didn't tolerate was disrespect. I would find out who the fuck he was, and I was going to finish the job. Just not here. His ass was going to feel me, real soon. The crowd was running, but I was getting a good look at this lil nigga's face, so I could find out exactly

who the fuck he is.

Danyelle Blakely

I could tell something was about to jump off when I saw Tico's jaw jumping. For as long as I've known him, he's never allowed anyone to talk to him crazy. That was one of the main reasons I was turned on by him. I don't know why, but I didn't expect him to shoot him in front of all these people. People were running around trying to get away, but this nigga was standing there like it was nothing. I knew it was an officer here because he was walking around questioning us when we first got here. Looking around, I saw him on the other side of the courts.

"Give me your gun." Tico was still staring the guy down, but I needed him to hear me. I'm sure the crowd wouldn't hold the officer back for long. "TICO! I need you to hear me. Give me your gun and get out of here. Come back to the house later." His ass took a minute to look up, but he finally passed it to me.

"Lil Mama-..." I cut him off when I saw the officer making his way over.

"Tico, you need to go. Now!" Not saying anything else, he took off. I watched him until I saw him jump in his car and drive off. Before I could do anything, I heard the officer.

"Freeze." I had no idea what was going on inside my head, but this wasn't what I had in mind. All I knew was I wanted Tico to get away, I didn't think about my dumb ass getting caught with the gun. Or what was going to happen though.

"Officer, this is a misunderstanding."

"So, you're saying you didn't just shoot this young man that's laying on the ground screaming in pain?" I didn't know what to say, so I didn't say anything. "Do you know who did it?" Hearing him say that had me thinking about Tico. I didn't want this to fall back on him. Dropping my head, I closed my eyes and made a decision.

"I did it officer." I thought the guy on the ground was going to protest, but his ass only screamed for an ambulance.

"Man fuck all that. Get me some help." The officer grabbed me and took the gun. Once he placed me in cuffs, he called for an ambulance. I had a million thoughts running through my mind, and I had no idea what I was getting myself into. I have never been in any trouble, so I was hoping for a slap on the wrist. I had no idea what to say, but I knew I couldn't tell them about Tico. It seemed like it took forever, but he finally put me in the back of the car and drove me to the station.

When I got inside, I looked around at everything. I had no idea how this was going to go, but I was scared out of my mind. We walked into a room, and I wanted to cry. On tv, they ask for a phone call, but I didn't know any numbers. Even if I did, Miesha wouldn't come get me. She would have probably told they ass to let me rot in here. I looked around the cold ass room and prayed this wasn't where I had to stay. The bench was metal, and they handcuffed me to it.

"Someone will be in here to talk to you soon." Before I could say anything, he left me in the holding room and was gone. I'm sure this was part of their tactic, and the shit was working. If it was anybody but Tico, my ass would be like the people on First 48. Eating a burger while snitching on everybody.

It seems like I was in here for hours, but I had no idea how long it has been. Someone finally walked in the door, and I was hoping they brought my chunky ass a doughnut or something. Grabbing the cuffs, he let me loose and grabbed me. We walked out the door and down the hall to another room and I had no idea what was about to happen when he sat me at a table and handcuffed me again.

"Can I please have something to drink?" The officer nodded and walked out the room. When he came back in, he had a burger and a can of Pepsi in his hand. I was about to tear that mufucka up, but I knew what that meant. They ass was about to try and get me to talk. His ass sat down and gave me a friendly smile.

"I know this is hard on you, but it won't be long. I'm sure you're hungry as well, so eat." I wanted to laugh in his face, but I grabbed the shit and took a big ass bite. My ass was barely chewing the shit was so good. "Now, I know you didn't shoot that gun. You don't deserve to go to jail behind this, so tell me what I want to know, and we'll get you out of here." His ass thought I was stupid. Nigga was talking to me like I didn't know the type of games they play.

"I told you it was me. I don't know what else you want me to say."

"Tell us your boyfriend's name. We know it wasn't you and we know you're protecting him. We won't let him know you told us. Just help us help you." Grabbing the Pepsi, I took a big gulp then let out a big dumb ass burp.

"Look at me. Do it seem like I got a boyfriend? The guy was bumping into me, and I told him to watch where he was going. He tried to fight me, and I defended myself. End of story." The lies came flying out and I hope they was buying them.

"Suit yourself. If you want to sit your dumb ass in jail for the rest of your life behind some nigga, that's on you." His ass snatched the burger and pop and walked out the room. Rolling my eyes, I sat back against the chair. His bitch ass could have let me finish eating. When I heard him say life, I wanted to cry and run the fuck up out of there, but I couldn't. To tell the truth is to tell on Tico and I just couldn't bring myself to do that.

An hour later, I was taken to booking and was fingerprinted. They were charging me with attempted murder, and it was nothing I could do about it. I'm not sure if I was ready to throw my life away, but I didn't have shit going for me. Yeah, it was dumb to take a charge for a nigga, but he was going to be something. I knew it and felt it in my gut; Tico was going to be that nigga and I couldn't take his life from him.

If I graduated high school, I still wouldn't have shit going for me. I was a nobody ass bum that had nothing. Hell, the only person I had in my life was Kema. She was gone ride with me, but I didn't have no one believing in me. Hell, we were cut from the same cloth, so neither of us had anything. I didn't know Tico's family, but I believed in him.

I know I wasn't his girl, but just like he looked out for me, I was now looking out for him. No matter how dumb the shit made me look. It wasn't much a mufucka could say about me, but I was solid. Yeah, being solid cost me my freedom, but sometimes you had to sacrifice for the person you loved. Besides, I know Tico is going to be there for me no matter how long I had to be in here, so I was good with my decision. I had to be. Nobody would understand my thought process, but I didn't have anyone to explain it to. It's not like he asked me to take the charge, so basically I did the shit to myself.

"I hope the low life is worth it. I see this so many times. Young girls come in here expecting their boyfriends to see them as a ride or die and end up looking dumb as fuck. That nigga is going to forget about you and move on to the next chick, while you throw your life away. Damn shame," a female officer said to me shaking her head.

I ignored her comment and waited to be taken to my next destination. She didn't know me, and I didn't owe her shit. This was my life and my decision. No one else would have to live with this shit, but me. I was going to get three meals a day and didn't have to worry about getting beat by Miesha. My ass would be with a roommate, just like I am now. Hell, it's ten of us in that mufucka and we can't do shit. Our ass walking around that bitch scared to breathe. I was in jail, just in a different form.

"See you in about twenty years." This time I laughed.

"Girl, you real pressed about my life. I mean, is you cool? Whatever decision I made is mine and mine alone. I'll be good. All I need for you to do is mind your business. Mmmk?" The bitch rolled her eyes and pushed me on the bus like I was nothing. Yeah, this was my life now, but it wasn't that different from the one I was already living.

Mantico St. Lauren

"Did you not hear what the fuck I said. I know what I said because I remember what the fuck I said when I fucking said it." Manny was talking to me like I was some lil nigga and he had me fucked up. I know I shouldn't have flipped out, but I wasn't about to start letting niggas come at me left.

"Look, I know man, but that lil nigga had that shit coming. I could have ended his life, but I didn't. I knew I couldn't afford that kind of heat, so I spared the lil nigga. For now." He looked at me in disbelief.

"Nigga, are you sure you ready to take over? I'm thinking maybe we moving this shit too fast." My mom's words were ringing in my ear.

"I'm ready. If I'm going to take over the city, you think it's not going to be mufuckas trying me? I have to nip it in the bud before it gets out of hand."

"That's not what I mean. If you going to shoot a nigga, then you kill his bitch ass. Dead men can't talk, and you left that nigga good and alive. You worried about witnesses when you left the main witness alive. The neighborhood will back you as long as you take care of them. Inflict fear, and then make sure they eat and you good. Son, I don't give a fuck who it is. If you pull that burner, you lay em down. No second chances and no witnesses. You feel me?" Nodding my head, I perfectly understood what he meant.

"Say less. Look, I know you run the city for now and you trying to be a father and shit, but I'mma need you to watch how you handle me. I'm a grown ass man with the city at my fingertips. Don't keep coming for me like that." This time, he nodded.

"I get that, but I'm still your father. You didn't know about me, but I knew about you. I've always dropped gems on you and if you did anything to jeopardize my money, I've always come for your head. You in yo feelings and shit and that's cool but keep that weak shit at home with yo lil bitches." This time I laughed.

"Nigga you got me fucked up. Ain't shit weak about me. I'm that nigga at home and in the streets. Yo old ass might could learn some shit from me. You can't even get some pussy you already had. Moms told me to tell you to get the fuck on." He laughed hard as hell.

"Yeah aight. As soon as I'm out the game, I'm going for what's mine. You wanna keep calling me Manny and that's cool. Somebody in that house about to be calling me daddy." I pushed his old ass and laughed.

"Hey, stop playing with me before I fuck you up. Naw but for real. It's not that I don't look at you as my pops. I've accepted that shit, but I've been calling you Manny for years and I'm just used to the shit. Calling you pops just seem like it will be forced. We good and I know who you are, be easy old nigga."

"This old nigga will lay your dumb ass out. We good. Now, get up out of my shit and go make me some bread. I need all I can get before I walk away." Shaking my head, I stood to leave out.

"I gotta go get my burner anyway before her ass end up having to sneak out the house." Manny threw his hand up stopping me with a shocked look on his face.

"Wait. You telling me you trusting yo life with some lil young bitch? Fuck you doing messing with a lil chick underage anyway? You should know better than that shit. You're a St. Lauren, you should be able to get some pussy from a grown bitch. I know I was fucking old hoes when I was your age."

"It ain't even like that. She just my lil homie and she solid. She the reason I got away from that shit both times. I trust her and it's not anybody out here that I can honestly say I trust."

"Aight, well bring her by here and let me see for myself. If my predecessor putting his life in her hands, I need to check her out."

"Manny, I said she good." It wasn't that I was ashamed of her because she wasn't my girl, but I didn't want her getting the wrong idea. If you take a chick to meet your parents, they thought they ass was in there.

"Aight, but you better make sure she is." His ass was always sending out threats, but that shit didn't move me. Not responding, I left out and jumped in my whip. It took me an hour to get to Dany's house, so it was kind of late when I got there. Getting out, I walked to the window and screamed her name. Instead of Dany, Kema stuck her head out.

"Hey Romeo, she not here. I'll be down in a second." I looked at my watch again to make sure I wasn't tripping, but it was after nine. I had no idea where her ass was at this time of night, but I got an uneasy feeling in my stomach. Kema opened the door slowly and tip toed onto the porch.

"What you mean she not here? Her ass better not be the fuck out here stealing and shit again."

"She gone and not coming back." Now I was confused. I know damn well Miesha didn't go against me and put her out or this time I was going to put her in a body bag.

"Fuck you mean she not coming back? Spit the shit out and quit talking in short sentences."

"The police stopped by the house earlier and told Miesha they charged her with attempted murder. They had to inform her because Dany is a minor. What the fuck happened?" I thought about earlier and I dropped my head.

"Fuck. I shot this nigga, and she took my burner. When she told me to leave, I didn't think shit of it. Everything went smooth last time, so I assumed she was good." Kema had fire in her eyes, and I couldn't blame her.

"You telling me you let my Best take a charge for you? She in jail and your cat eyed ass around here free. Wow. You're a fuck boy and I don't know what she sees in your ass. Get the fuck off our porch."

"Hey, I know you pissed, but don't forget who the fuck you talking to. I didn't ask her to do a muthafucking thing and I didn't know none of this went down. I'mma fix it but watch yo tone talking to me. What's her last name, so I can figure this shit out?"

"Danyelle Blakely is her name. You better get my Best out this shit." Running down the stairs, I got in the car and tried to think of my next move. Making sure I didn't fuck up, I grabbed my phone and called Manny.

"Hey, I need your help. Shorty got caught with my heat and took the charge for me. I need to know how I get her out this shit."

"I know you don't want to hear this, but you have to let her ride this out. If you go down there and try to do anything, your name is attached to the case. I'm sure they know she didn't do the shit and she won't talk. They looking for a mufucka to come show their face, so they can link you to it. If you don't hear shit else I say, don't do anything. She knew what she was doing, and she made her decision. If she has no priors, she won't do that much time." I looked at the phone and then put it back to my ear.

"So, you good with me leaving her in there to rot for some shit she didn't do. That don't sit right with me Manny."

"I know son. It's fucked up when someone you cool with gets caught up in the crossfire. This is the life we live and that's the reason Yvette didn't want anything to do with it. I understood and that's why I never held it against her. Sometimes good people get fucked up behind our shit."

"So, I just say fuck shorty even though she fucked her life up for me? When she gets out, life gone be hard for her with a felony." I could hear him blowing out a breath, so I was sure he was trying not to go off.

"Look, if you care about the girl or what happens to her make sure she straight when she gets out. Money, house, and a car. That will make yall even. Unless you want to go down and lose your spot at the throne, listen to what I'm saying."

"Say less." Hanging up, leaned my head back and closed my eyes. I didn't want to say fuck Dany, but what was the alternative? Me going down and then someone else taking over my city. Hell, I fought for this shit, and it was going to be mine. Fuckkkk. I had no choice but to listen to Manny on this one. Whenever Dany got out, I was going to make sure she was set all the way up. She would never have to ask nobody

for nothing.

Danyelle Blakely

CURRENT DAY 2021...

"Blakely, you have a visitor." I looked confused because
I had no idea who would be here to see me. Sliding on my
shower shoes, I stood up and followed the officer out. When I
first got here, I used to think Tico would come and visit me.
Kema told me he came by the house, so I knew that he knew I
was in here. Days turned into weeks, weeks turned into
months, and months turned into years. Tico never came to
see me and at first I was crushed, but I was over that shit now.

A bitch was stronger, and I didn't need that nigga.
Yeah, it's fucked up he couldn't even come say thank you to
the mufucka that took a charge for him, but it was a decision
that I made. I was at the end and on tomorrow, I would be
walking out these doors. I was going to start a new chapter of
my life and Tico or the thought of him wasn't in it. Seeing
Kema sitting at the table, I was confused on why she was here.

"Hey Best; you do know I get out tomorrow right? So why your ass here today?"

"I ain't have shit to do, so I came for the weekend. I didn't want to get up early in the morning to drive the three hours it was going to take to get to you. I'm not a morning person and you know that." Laughing, I hugged her and took a seat.

"Well, I'm glad I don't have to wait on your ass. A bitch is ready to go. If I eat another noodle I'mma die in this mufucka."

"Girl, remember the days we used to beg for some noodles? I can't wait for you to come home. We popping bottles and eating everything that ain't tied down. That lil weight you lost gone come back in no time." Even though I was never insecure, I love how I look now. I worked out every day, and I finally got my shit balanced out. I was still thick as hell, but it was finally proportioned right.

"Chile, the only thing I'm trying to do is find a job as soon as I get out. Being homeless ain't a good look." She laughed, but I was dead ass serious.

"Girl, you sound crazy. I wish the fuck I would let you live on a park bench. You can sleep on my floor." This time I laughed hard as hell. Even though that was a pissy ass offer, it was better than nowhere at all.

"I know I shouldn't be asking this, but have you seen him? Did you tell him I'm coming home?"

"Girl, have you lost your mind? Don't be asking me about that clown ass nigga. I got some dick lined up for you as soon as you touch down. I know your wrist bout tired as shit. You been playing in that pussy for too long." I looked around to make sure the guard didn't hear her, but from the way he was laughing, I knew he had.

"Girl, shut the fuck up. You still don't have no sense. Can't take yo ugly ass nowhere. You know damn well I'm a virgin, so I'm not about to be fucking no random ass nigga. Just get me a good vibrator and I'm good."

"I got you Best. I'm about to get up out of here and go find me some food. I can't wait until tomorrow. We going out and we gone tear the fucking city up. My Best bitch is coming home." She did a scream and a little dance. I couldn't do shit but join in with her. Walking back to my room, I had a big ass smile on my face. I was finally about to go home, and it was time for me to shake some shit up. That nigga thought he was gone leave me in here to rot and that shit was going to fly. He had me fucked up. That nigga thought he was the king, but it was time for that nigga to fall off the throne.

****

"Bessttttt, you're free bitch." I almost fell I took off running so fast. Jumping in her arms, I hugged her hard and tight. Even though I didn't feel like I was about to cry, the tears started flowing from my eyes. "Awww, don't cry. You know how ugly you are when your ass get to doing that shit."

"Shut the fuck up. I can't believe how good you look. Plus, look at your whip, I see you bitch." She was in a black on black Mercedes Benz GLE. This bitch was nice. I walked around it and smiled hard as hell for her. We climbed inside and I was still smiling. "I'm proud of you Best, and I know I've said it a million times, but thank you." My girl stood by me the entire bid and I was grateful to her. She didn't miss a week visiting me and I could never repay her.

"You know how we get down. Ain't no way I was gone leave you in that bitch by yourself. I'mma always have your back." She slid on a pair of Fendi glasses and passed me a pair. "I can't have you out here looking a mess. We gotta go shopping and get you some clothes."

"I know you told me you were doing well, but what the fuck is it that you do? You out here living like a hustler's wife. What's up?"

"Just know I'm getting my coins. Mmmk." We talked and laughed all the way back to Chicago like we never missed a beat. She didn't have to fill me in on shit because she did that every time she came to visit me. My girl stood beside me, and I swear I loved her ass for it.

As soon as we touched down, she took me to the mall and spent a bag on me. It felt funny having her do all this for me, but I knew I needed it. I wasn't in the position to turn shit down, so I smiled and allowed her to spoil me. Whatever she was doing for a living, I wanted in on it, so I can try to get some money. A bitch really was homeless even though I knew Kema had my back, I didn't want to be living off her for too long. We had eaten and we were finally done and driving to her house.

As soon as we pulled up, my mouth hit the floor. Her house was a block long and looked like some shit off tv. Either this hoe hit the lottery, she was sucking a rich nigga's dick, or her ass was selling drugs. I don't think I've ever even seen a house that looked this nice. Kema cut the car off and handed me the keys.

"I'll be back to get you later. We're going out, so get pretty bitch." I looked at her confused as I grabbed my bags.

"Okay, but why are you giving me your keys. I don't have a license and I don't know how to drive."

"It's yours. Make yourself at home, I'll be back." She jumped in a Benz C Class and drove off before I could respond. I had no idea what to say, but I was gone have to find a way to repay her. That bitch could have come in and showed me around, but I wasn't complaining. Making sure I had all my bags; I went to the door and tried the knob. Seeing it was unlocked, I walked inside. I thought I was prepared for how nice it looked, but the inside had me floored. This bitch was ugly paid, and I immediately removed my shoes. I didn't want to mess up her marble floors with my dirty ass jail shoes. It was a long winding staircase that led upstairs from the foyer. I didn't know which way to go to look at the rest of the house, but I was about to run all over this bitch.

"Welcome home." The hairs stood up on my arms and I was frozen in place. I would never forget the sound of his voice; I just had no idea what he was doing here. Out of nowhere, it hit me. Him and Kema must be fucking around. My heart fell to my ass and then the anger flowed through my veins. I was going to jail for the rest of my life, because these

two bitches was dead.

Mantico St. Lauren

I don't know why, but I was nervous as fuck waiting on Kema to bring Dany to my house. I know it was no way to make up for me not checking on her, but I was damn sure gone try. I just didn't want to see that disappointed look in her eyes. My ass wasn't expecting her to look so damn sexy. Jail had done Lil Mama good, and I could see she used her time wisely.

Her thickness that was once sloppy, was now curvy and sticking out in all the right places. That ass was sitting heavy, and her hair was now down her back. She was looking around when I finally spoke up. Instead of the disappointed look, anger washed over her face, and she charged at me like a linebacker. I had no idea what the fuck she was about to do, until she hit me.

I knew she was going to be pissed, but Lil Mama had me fucked up. Grabbing her, I slammed her against the wall. Her chest was heaving up and down and she was staring at me like she wanted to kill my ass. I opened my mouth to say something, but her crazy ass leaned in and bit me. Mufucka had a grip on my shit like a rabid ass Pitbull. I couldn't pull away or her ass was going to rip a hole out my shit.

"Dany, let my shit go before I shoot yo ass." She released me, but I could tell she was still pissed.

"Go ahead. Maybe you got another dumb bitch sitting around willing to take a case for you, and while they gone, you fuck they best friend and leave them to rot."

"I'm sorry I didn't-... Wait, what? I ain't fuck your friend, what the fuck you talking about?" I let her go, but I could tell I had to watch her ass. She was still looking at me like she wanted to fight.

"Why the fuck you in her house then? I'm not slow Tico. Plus, how she getting all this money?" I couldn't do shit but laugh.

"Nigga, this my shit. She had strict instructions on what to do when she picked you up. She didn't tell you that was your truck and shit?" She looked confused.

"Yeah, but I thought she was giving it to me."

"Naw, Lil Mama. I bought the truck and gave her the money to take you shopping. Kema getting bread since she works for me, but I set you up. I figured I owed you that much. I appreciate what you did, so I wanted to make sure you were good when you got out."

"So, what I'm supposed to do sleep in my car? I can't even drive, dumb ass." I tried my best not to go off on her ass, but she was pushing my buttons.

"I wanted you to pick out your own crib, but you got that coming too. I even got some bread put up for you. Look, I couldn't come see you, but I got you." Her anger turned to nervousness. She started shifting from foot to foot.

"So, I have to live here with you?" She sounded pissed off about it.

"I mean, just for a second if you want to. I would like you to, so you can catch me up on everything and I can let you know what's been going on with me. If you not good with that, you can stay with Kema."

"I'll let you know. Can you show me where I can sleep for now? I want to take a nap before me and Kema go out tonight."

"Yeah, come on. Did she tell you that it's my party you coming to?" I could see the look on her face that she didn't want to go. "It's my birthday." I saw her face soften and I knew she was gone hang out with a nigga.

"Okay. I guess I'll come for a little while." Walking her upstairs, I took her to my guest room and her mouth hit the floor. I can tell she was impressed, and a nigga was proud of everything I've accomplished. I was finally the king of the city, and I was on top of the world. She had no idea how grateful I would always be to her, hell, she was the reason any of this was possible.

"This is really nice Tico. I'm glad your dreams came true." I could hear some disappointment in her voice, and I guess it was time to address the elephant in the room.

"Look, I just want to thank you for everything you did Lil Mama. You're the reason I got any of this and I want you to know you straight. I got you." A hint of anger crossed her face and then smiled.

"You got me huh? You think you would have had me when I was locked the fuck up for yo ass but do yo thang. It's King now isn't it?"

"Don't do that. I couldn't allow my name to get caught up in that shit. I know what you did was a lot, and I'm telling you I appreciate that shit."

"And I'm telling you I don't give a fuck about your appreciation. Now, if you don't mind, can you leave so I can take a nap." Since I didn't want to curse her the fuck out, I nodded and left the room. Heading downstairs, I grabbed her bags and took them back up to her room. Not wanting to just walk in, I knocked. When she didn't respond, I opened the door. Dany was sitting on the bed with her head in her hands crying.

"You good?" Her head snapped up and I regretted saying anything.

"What the fuck. Didn't I ask you to leave?"

"Look, I just brought yo bags back and I saw you was crying. I get that you hurt, but you not about to disrespect me in my own shit. Get yo emotions in check, before I do it for you." I walked out and slammed the door, but all I really wanted to do was hug her. Lil Mama been through a lot, and what she did for me didn't make her life any better. Fuck. Walking to my room, I sat on the bed and laid back. Since I've been on top, my days have been less stressful. Lil Mama ain't been here twenty minutes and I was already stressed the fuck out.

****

Deciding to go with my yellow diamond set, I put my earrings, chain, and Rolex on. It was a hot summer night, so I had on a black Burberry polo shirt, some black jean shorts, and my yellow and black Burberry gym shoes. Yeah, it was my party, but I wasn't the type to dress up. Grabbing my wallet and my keys, I walked out the room to see if Dany was ready. Knocking on her door, I waited for her to answer.

"Yeah."

"Hey, I'll be downstairs. We gotta head out soon; a nigga can't be late for his own shit. Hurry the fuck up." When she didn't respond, I headed downstairs. Ten minutes later, right when I was about to lose my patience, I saw her out the corner of my eye. Turning around, I had to convince my dick not to brick up. Dany had on a black one piece short set. It wasn't the spandex type of thing, but very classy even though it was fitting her body just right. I'm guessing Kema helped her pick out the colors for my party, because she had on some yellow YSL heels. We were matching to a tee, but she wasn't my date. Her hair was pulled up in a bun and she had no make up on her face. Just lip gloss.

"Ummm, you ready." Dany broke my trance, so I got myself together.

"Yeah. Let's go." When she made it over to me, I put my hand on the nape of her back as I eased her outside to my Lambo.

"I thought Kema was coming back to take me to the party. Why the fuck do I have to ride with you?" I took a deep breath and tried not to go the fuck off.

"It didn't make sense for her to drive an hour out of her way when we both were going to the same fucking place. If you got a problem with being in my presence, you could have stayed the fuck at home. Today is my birthday, and I'm not about to let you fuck that shit up with yo Debbie Downer attitude. So, sit back, shut the fuck up, and when we get there try to have a good time." She opened her mouth but closed it back. Tired of going back and forth with her, I ignored her the rest of the way. On the outside, we looked like a great fucking unit. You would think we were a power couple, even though we weren't together. No matter how we looked, we were not good. It was so much tension in the air, I could cut it with my dick.

We finally pulled up to the space I rented out downtown and I couldn't be happier. Stepping outside, I passed my keys to the valet and walked over to Dany's side. I could tell she didn't want to be here, but I was over her attitude. I was ready to enjoy myself, and she could go do her own thing. Opening her door, I waited for her to climb out, and headed inside. As soon as I walked in everybody started raising their glasses and screaming. Not wanting them to know Dany ruined my mood, I put on a fake smile and waved at everyone. Walking over to VIP, I took a seat and immediately grabbed a bottle.

"Hey nigga, you trying it tonight ain't you?" I looked at Mink confused trying to figure out what the fuck he meant.

"What you mean?"

"You gone bring two bitches to the same party? I know you that nigga, but that's some messy shit." Even though me and Dany wasn't together, I looked around trying to spot Celeste.

"Don't get nervous now. You knew damn well she was coming. It's yo fucking birthday party; what you thought." Fil made sense, but I was good.

"Lil Mama just cool. I'm good." Even though Dany was in VIP with us, she was sitting on the other side trying to be as far from me as possible.

"Hey nigga. Ain't that the lil fat chick from back in the day?" Mink looked at her to see what Fil was talking about and started laughing.

"Well I'll be damned. That is her. I thought you ain't want shorty. I'm not gone lie, she done came a long way. Hell, I'll fuck the shit out of her. You say yall just cool?" We all laughed, but I didn't find the shit funny for real. Naw, I didn't want her, but she was off limits.

"She don't want yall dusty asses. All that ass on the floor, you looking at the one you think fat." Mink shrugged his shoulders.

"Hey, I tend to like fat bitches and fat asses."

"Nigga, shut the fuck up." I was about to get up and ask Dany if she wanted a drink when Celeste came into VIP. I prayed nothing kicked off, but I'm sure my luck not that good.

Danyelle Blakely

Sitting there, I felt so out of place. Kema needed to

hurry the fuck up, or I was getting the fuck out of here. I don't

know why Tico and his friends didn't know I could hear them,

but I could. I was already uncomfortable when the prettiest

woman I've ever seen walked in VIP. She was tall and slim

with the longest legs I've ever seen. It seemed like them

bitches went on for days. Her weave was to her thighs, and

her light skin and pouty lips were perfect.

"Damn baby, it took you long enough. Why were you

late to your own party?" For some reason, Tico seemed

nervous, but he stood to hug her. Of course, she leaned in for

a kiss and my ass was jealous as fuck. Yeah, I was mad at Tico

for now, but I would always love that nigga. Not about to sit

here and watch this shit, I stood up and walked over to him.

"Can you call Kema for me, please?" He looked as if he

wanted to kill me for my timing, but I didn't give a fuck.

"Yeah, give me a minute."

"Ummm, excuse me. Who the fuck is this?" I started laughing hard as fuck.

"Tico, call Kema. Now!" I could see the anger in his face, but he grabbed his phone out of his pocket.

"Am I invisible? I said, who the fuck is this bitch?"

"Celeste, calm that shit down. This my homie Dany, she good. Now relax before I fuck yo ass up." Still pissed at Tico, I decided to fuck his shit up.

"Yeah, relax bitch." Before anyone could respond, Kema walked up hype as hell.

"Bessstttttt, let's get this party the fuck started. Where the fucking liquor at Tico?" I smiled as I walked over to her and hugged her tight.

"You're the king of the fucking city, but you're entertaining these ghetto ass bitches. I thought this was going to be a classy event, you could have kept me out of this shit," this wanna be boujie ass bitch said.

"I didn't invite you. I'm that nigga, I didn't ask nobody to be in this bitch. If you feeling a way, you can leave or go sit the fuck down Celeste. I'm not doing this shit."

"Wow." She stormed off as me and Kema fell the fuck out laughing.

"Let me guess, she mad yo big booty ass over here with her nigga?"

"Yeah Kema. You could have told me this nigga had a bitch. You seemed to leave that out every time you came to catch me up. Oh, and why the fuck didn't you tell me that was his house, and this was his party?"

"Because I wanted you to get some surprise dick. Did you get some? Never mind. I'm sure you didn't or you wouldn't be in this bitch with an attitude. Best is here now, so let's turn this shit the fuck up. Tico, pass me that bottle. It's yo birthday, but it's my girl's first day back." I thought he would go running behind Celeste, but he didn't. He passed Kema the bottle after pouring himself a cup.

An hour later, we all were having a good time. Tico and his boys just watched the women as they drank and hit the woods. Me and Kema, was drunker than a bitch and I had no regrets. I didn't touch the weed, because I had no idea when I was gone have to see my PO officer. Since I was feeling myself and I was single, I walked over to one of the niggas sitting with Tico and started dancing. Kema did the same and we was fucking it up.

"Besssttt. Let me find out you learned how to throw that thang in there. Them bitches was making you strip for them, huh?" I laughed and kept shaking my ass like I wanted something to fall out that bitch. I glanced at Tico, and he was fuming. I don't know why, his ass don't want me and he got a bitch.

"Hey, this ass is fat. I might have to hit this shit tonight." Before I could respond to the guy I was dancing on, I felt a pinch that almost pulled my skin off. Jumping up, I turned around fast as fuck with tears in my eyes. I couldn't even respond before Tico grabbed me around my neck like I was some little rag doll.

"Why the fuck you disrespecting me?"

"Brother, I don't think she can answer. You kind of snatched her throat through her ass. What? I'm just saying. You might wanna get her a trach or something." I was trying to look at her and say bitch shut the fuck up and help me, but the only thing my eyes was giving was I'm about to die.

"Shut the fuck up Kema. Bring yo disrespectful ass the fuck on. Party over." My ass was coughing trying to catch my breath, but the shit wasn't coming.

"Wait, so you shutting down the party because I was about to get some pussy and yo bitch left?" I had no idea who the guy was talking, but I felt sorry for him.

"Nigga. I told you if I brought you to this party to sit the fuck down and shut the fuck up. Now yo dumb ass about to die." One of the guys that was calling me fat said. All I knew was, I wasn't about to take another case for his bitch ass, so I ran out of VIP holding my throat. Kema was right on my heels.

"Bitch, where the fuck are you going?"

"Get me out of here. This nigga crazy as hell. When I catch my breath, I'mma beat his ass." She looked at me with her mouth turned up.

"How you gone beat his ass if you gone sis? Make it make sense. Come on, I guess you can go to my house. I was trying to get some dick tonight, but I guess you will do. You probably riding for our side of the fence anyway." We both laughed hard as hell as we walked outside.

"You tried it. If I was eating pussy, I wouldn't want yours. Best, your shit been ran through since we was kids. You can keep them wobbly walls." Stumbling and drunk, we walked towards her car.

"I went on a hiatus for a year friend. My shit grew back. I only have a one bedroom, so when I have company over, you gotta get yo ass on the couch."

"That's fine friend. Just let me know when someone coming over. Thank you for everything." We climbed inside her car as she drove off.

"I wish yo soft ass stop thanking me. I did what I was supposed to. Hell, you would have done it for me. It's plenty of nights you saved me from that bitch." That had me thinking, so I turned to face her.

"Whatever happened to Miesha?"

"Bitch, I don't know. One night, she didn't come home. Tico started coming over, well, him or his boys making sure we ate every day. When I turned eighteen, I asked him for a job, and he put me on. I know you mad at him, but maybe you should hear him out. He had to have a good reason why he left you in there like that. I could tell it bothered him and he made sure he asked about you every time I came back from visiting." I looked at her and she was pleading with me to hear him out with her eyes.

"Girl, fuck him. He tried to tell me that bullshit ass story, but I ain't want to hear it. Nothing he says can make up for what he did. As soon as he gets me my house, I'm done with his bitch ass."

"Well, that's going to be hard to do. This nigga is blocking traffic and pointing a gun at our ass." I looked towards the street and sure enough his ass was standing there looking sexy and crazy as the same damn time.

"Dear God, help me and my pussy make it." Kema laughed, but I didn't find shit funny.

Mantico St. Lauren

When I realized Dany had left against my wishes, I turned towards the lil nigga that was running his mouth. Grabbing my gun, I placed it at his temple. Fil stood up and moved away from him quick as hell.

"Damn, you not gone even try to save yo nigga?" Mink asked him shaking his head as he moved out my way as well.

"Hell naw, I told his dumb ass. Niggas be having to learn the hard way." Not wanting to hear shit else, I pulled the trigger.

"Get this shit cleaned up. I was trying to have a peaceful night, and yall bring this bitch ass nigga in my shit."

"I mean. How was we supposed to know you was bringing yo other girl? That you saying not yo girl. When yo other girl was here. If she off limits, say that shit. I almost slid her my number." When Mink saw how I looked at him, he threw his hands up. "I'm just saying."

"Just don't say shit. She ain't my girl, but she ain't for yall either. Are we clear?" They nodded, but I had no idea why I was blocking lil mama from getting a nigga. We were just friends, and I had a girl. I'm not gone say I love Celeste, because I don't, but we work. I met her a year ago through the connect and we been rocking ever since. I still fucked other bitches, but her sex was decent. Normally, she didn't question shit I did or said. Hell, I've never even heard her talk like she did tonight. So, I know she was intimidated by Dany. At the end of the day, I was that nigga, and she wasn't going to disrespect me. Especially not in front of anyone else. Disrespect my dick if you gone open yo mouth to me.

Now, I had to deal with another chick thinking she could go against what the fuck I said. They were looking at me crazy, as I stood there with my gun pointed at Kema's car. I knew she wouldn't cross me because I'm the one that fed her. However, Dany was her Best, so she might try the shit. Cocking my gun back, I let her know I was about to let this bitch ride when Dany got out of the car. She walked over to me stumbling with an attitude.

"What the fuck you want Tico?" Grabbing her by her neck, I dragged her to my car and pushed her inside.

"The next time I say do something, you fucking do it. Slow ass storming the fuck out like you run some shit." She looked at me like I was crazy, but she didn't say shit. I couldn't even tell you why I was so mad, but I was. Lil Mama had me fucked up. Driving off fast as hell in my Lambo, I headed towards the house.

"I don't want to cause you and your girl problems. So, I was gone just stay at Kema's house. I'm not trying to be a burden." I don't know why she insisted on playing with me, but I wasn't in the mood for her shit. Not responding, I kept driving towards my crib. I hadn't told Celeste about Dany yet, but I would cross that bridge when I get there.

An hour later, we were pulling up at the crib and I jumped out pissed off. When I didn't hear her heels, I turned around to make sure she was following me. Dany was walking slowly and with an attitude, but she was coming. Opening the door, I walked inside and went straight to the bar. Downing my first drink, I poured another and waited for her to walk through the door.

"You want a drink?"

"Do you want to leave me the fuck alone." She tried to mumble it, but I heard her loud and clear. I was about to treat her life, when she tried to walk off, but her heels went one way, and her ankles went another. I wanted to laugh hard as hell, but she started crying. Walking over towards her, I grabbed her ankle to look at it. "Ouch, damn." In one second, her ass was going to be climbing up the stairs on her fucking knees.

"You pushing it Dany." Scooping her in my arms, I picked her up and carried her up the stairs. She leaned in and sniffed me, and I had to look at her like she was crazy. "Did you just smell my neck? Don't come home on that weird shit."

"I've always wondered what you smelled like. Mmmmm, back door and cologne. Shit got me feeling some type of way."

"It's called back woods Lil Mama. You drunk as fuck. It's okay though, I got you." I pushed her door open and walked inside. Sitting her on the bed, I went over to her dresser and looked through them. I couldn't do shit but shake my head when I realized she didn't buy anything to sleep in. Leaving out, I ran to my room and grabbed one of my shirts and went back to her room. Lil Mama was snoring like some big burly ass nigga with her mouth open. Leaning down, I unhooked her heels and took them off. Her feet wasn't done, but they were naturally pretty. I realized I was still holding them and let them go. Shaking my head at myself, I took a deep breath.

"Dany, what the fuck you got me in here doing?" Looking her short set over, I saw it zipped in the back. Pushing her over, I unzipped it and removed the jumper from her body. The way her titty plopped out when I pulled it down had me wishing my face was right there. Them bitches was big, firm, and perky. Her nipples were so round and perfect it took everything in me not to trace my finger around them.

Not trying to be on no creep shit, I continued to pull them off and her pussy jumped out at my ass. I forgot shorty was in jail and they must don't allow razors. Lil Mama had a big ol wolf pussy. You couldn't even see where her slit began it was so fucking hairy. After she was completely naked, I pulled the shirt over her head and pulled her all the way in the bed. Outside of her pussy looking like a nappy head nigga named Bill, her body was perfect. I knew I shouldn't be looking at her in that way, but I couldn't help it.

Even if I wanted to fuck her, how could I fix my mouth to say some shit like that to her? In her eyes, I was the villain in her story. I'm not gone lie; Dany done grew the fuck up. I could see why that nigga was all one her ass, but I refused to let another nigga hurt her. Granted, I was the first nigga to inflict hurt on her, but the shit wasn't intentional. I was gone try to make it up to her, but Lil Mama may never forgive me and that was something I had to live with.

That was one piece of advice I wasn't sure I should have taken from Manny, but it was too late for regrets. My life was perfect, and a nigga had made it. If I hadn't listened to Manny, it's no telling where I would be. Shit was one of those catch twenty twos. Besides, I didn't ask Dany to do that shit. Yeah, I owed her everything, but she did that shit on her own accord. Leaving out her room, I went to mine and took my clothes off.

Jumping in the shower, I tried to relax to relieve some of the stress I could feel taking over. Even though Dany wasn't going to be staying here long, it was going to go the fuck down as soon as Celeste found out what was going on. I was gone have to take her on a trip or something to smooth this shit over. Grabbing a towel, I left the bathroom and climbed in my bed.

I had no idea what the fuck went through my mind, but first thing in the morning I was going to look for Dany a place to stay. With the body she had on her, it was best I kept

her as far away as possible. I didn't need the drama right now.

Closing my eyes, I tried to fall asleep, but all I could see was

Dany's perfect ass body.

Waking up, I looked around trying to figure out where I was. Noticing I was in my temporary bed undressed, had me wondering what the fuck happened last night. I know I was drunk, but I didn't think I was that drunk. Placing my hand between my legs, I didn't feel any pussy juices or blood flowing down my legs, so I kind of figured out I was good. Smelling bacon frying, I headed downstairs. Seeing Celeste standing at the stove with a frown on her face, I couldn't do shit but shake my head.

"Hey babe, I decided to come over and fix you breakfast. I know I did the most last night, but I'm sorry. I should have known better. Big ain't even your type. Anyway-..." She finally looked up and realized I wasn't Tico. When she realized it was the "big bitch" her mouth hit the floor.

"I mean, since you came over uninvited you could have at least asked if I liked my shit light, dark, or fluffy." She didn't find the shit funny, but I couldn't control my laugh.

Walking over to the stove, I grabbed a piece. "It's a lil burnt, but it will do. Call me when the shit done. My name Danyelle, well Tico calls me Dany. Either way, it's not big bitch. Mmmk?" Not giving her a chance to answer me, I walked off leaving her looking dumb. I knew it was about to go down, so I took a bite of my bacon smiling as I went back to my room.

Hopefully, after the argument he was about to have, Tico would take me to Kema's. So, I decided to get ready and wait. Walking in the bathroom, I turned on the shower water as I put the last piece of bacon in my mouth. I could hear screaming, so I laughed as I pulled the shirt over my head and climbed in. This water felt way better than the hard ass water we had in jail. Fake ass soap and dingy ass metal stalls. You couldn't even go in that bitch barefoot or you was gone come out that mufucka with a fungus.

Holding my head under the water, I thought about masturbating but decided against it. I've done that shit for three years; I was tired of flicking that mufucka. It would have been nice to come home to some welcome back dick, but I guess a truck I couldn't drive was nice.

"Dany, where you at Lil Mama?" I could faintly hear Tico talking to me, but I wasn't with his shit today. Nigga was around here acting like I did something to him and shit. "Fuck." I could hear him inside the bathroom now and I became shy as hell. I knew I had gotten my body tight, but this was the first time a man has seen me naked.

"If you don't mind, I would like to take a shower in peace. I'm sure yo girl gone really flip her shit if she finds out you in here staring at my ass." He had the nerve to scoff and laugh.

"And she will let the shit go when she sees your pussy got dude in a chokehold. You need to get that shit waxed or something. Straight up. Shit ain't natural." I looked down and back up at him and I didn't know what to say.

"Fuck you Tico. How about that. If you so disgusted by me, why the fuck you still standing there looking? Get out. I'll come get you when I'm ready for you to drop me off."

"You mean as fuck. You don't need no dick or nothing do you? Yo ass just got out of jail, so I'm sure you backed the fuck up." Since he wanted to take it there, I decided to gut punch his ass.

"I was trying to get some last night, but you was cock blocking. Get the fuck out my shit Tico. I need to wash my ass and dry off." Just like I thought, he shut the fuck up and walked out. I handled my hygiene and grabbed a towel. When I stepped inside the room, he was still there waiting around on me. Rolling my eyes, I went to my drawer to find something to throw on.

"All this back and forth needs to stop. Now, Celeste is downstairs waiting on me to properly introduce yall. I need you to act like you got some fucking sense. I know you mad at me, but I need you to do this for me." Smiling, I nodded my head.

"I got you. Just let me get dressed first." His ass actually smiled and walked out like shit was sweet. Knowing she was still here, I grabbed some leggings that I knew was going to have my ass sitting heavy, and a cropped t-shirt. I got dressed and threw on my Burberry sneakers I purposely got because I saw him in them a few years ago. I knew they were probably old, but the lady said they were classics. So, I was guessing they didn't go out of style. Pulling my hair into a bun, I applied some lip gloss and headed downstairs.

I made sure my ass was bouncing hard as hell. I found them in the front sitting on the couch. Making sure I gave that bitch everything I was supposed to give, I sat down and waited to see what was up.

"Celeste, this is my homie Dany. She just got out of jail, and she did a bid for me. It's only right that I look after her. Once we find her a house, everything will be back to normal. I just need yall to be easy until that happens. We good?" Celeste looked at me and smirked.

"Baby, why didn't you say she was just one of those bitches that moves drugs in her fat ass or take cases for niggas. I know you like classy chicks, so it's no problem here. It's very nice to meet you Dany." I looked at Tico and his dumb ass just sat there looking shocked. This nigga had me fucked up.

"Tico, why didn't you tell me you was fucking this hungry bitch. I mean, I can see why you just came in the shower with me, you tired of looking at this skinny bitch. I know you really want thick bitches, so it's no problem here. I'm Danyelle, it's very nice to meet you dummy." Tico dropped his head, and Celeste jumped up like she was ready to fight.

"This bitch gotta go. I'm not about to be disrespected in my own shit." Tico finally looked at her like she was crazy.

"First off, this my shit. Secondly, you came in this bitch being disrespectful. I already told you, I won't have that shit. Now, you already know how the fuck I am, so I have no idea why the fuck you trying me. Watch yo mouth and respect my fucking company. I gotta take her to handle some business, so you can see yourself out. I'll be to holla at you later." This bitch rolled her eyes and stomped out. I had no idea how she didn't break her legs how hard she was walking. Laughing, I stood up and went to the kitchen. Grabbing a plate, I helped myself to some of the bitch's food.

"Dany, what the fuck was that? You not my girl Lil Mama and I don't do messy shit. You on that bullshit with me, when all I'm trying to do is make this shit right. What's up?"

"I'm not your responsibility and I'm done being your charity case. You don't owe me shit. Yo bitch is disrespectful. I've dealt with bullies like her all my life, no more. If you don't want me to knock her the fuck out, keep her away from me. Matter of fact, you can stay the fuck away from me and go be happy. Like you said, I'm not yo girl. Fuck you steady acting like I am for?"

"When did I act like you was my bitch? Because I'm helping you? Grow the fuck up."

"Naw, when you got mad I was about to fuck yo boy and you did the most. You grow up. I don't belong to you Tico. At this point, we not even friends. I like to eat by myself these days, so if you don't mind." I could tell he wanted to fight, but I was tired of him. Tico has never given me the impression that he wanted me, but he knew I wanted him. So, why the fuck he keeps playing in my face and shit?

"I'm not trying to beef with you. This is not what I wanted. I saw this shit going differently, but I been fucking up since you came home. Just give me a few days Lil Mama, and I'll be out of yo life." Letting the frown in my face relax, I nodded.

"Okay but can you either get a plate or get the fuck out my face. You look like you bout ready to steal my shit?" Laughing, he walked towards the door.

"Man, hurry the fuck up." I couldn't stop the smile that spread across my face. That nigga just did some things to me. Whew, grabbing my fork I continued to eat my food. For that bitch to be so skinny, she damn sure could cook. Eggs was fluffy as shit.

Mantico St. Lauren

"Where else we going Tico?" For someone that sat in jail for three years, she damn sure didn't have any patience. We only went to get her I.D and stopped at her parole officer. She doesn't know it, but I paid that nigga off, so she didn't have to check in and shit. I wanted her to be able to live her life without a constant reminder of what she went through.

"I wanted to show you the city through my eyes, but first, we gotta make a stop." She rolled her eyes, and I couldn't do shit but shake my head.

"Just know if you keep me out all day, you feeding me." I swear all this girl has ever done since I've known her was talk about food. I see ain't shit changed. When I parked the car, her mouth dropped open. "Nigga, you trying to be funny or something?"

"Naw, but that shit dead ass gotta come off. You around this bitch like you about to do some seventies porn. The shit ain't cute and your body too banging for that." I had pulled up to this waxing place and Lil Mama was offended as fuck.

"For a nigga that don't want me, you sure are concerned with my shit. You sure you don't want a taste?" I don't know why, but her question had me thrown off. I've never looked at her like that, but I couldn't help but think about her body.

"Naw, but you still represent my name mufucka. Everybody know you my lil homie, so you can't be out here trying to fuck with that shit between yo legs. Now, shut the fuck up and bring yo ass on." She grabbed my hand and pulled me back in the car.

"Wait, you're going in with me?" She looked nervous.

"Yeah, trust me. You gone need somebody in there to hold yo hand. That shit gone hurt like hell. It's a lot of hair down there." She was still nervous, but she allowed me to get out the car this time. Dany was following behind me close as hell and I wanted to ask here where was all that tough shit now. I already called ahead, so she was immediately taken in the back. I wanted to record her, but if I pulled my phone out, I knew she was going to lose her shit. Seeing her with her legs propped open, had my dick waking up. Trying not to stare, I looked down in my phone and tried to act like I was doing something. As soon as the wax was applied, I grabbed her hand because I knew how that shit was about to go.

"Aww hell naw. Bitch, I will beat yo mutha fucking ass. Did you just cut me?" I laughed under my breath, but that shit was funny as fuck. When she got to her lips, I thought Dany had gotten used to it.

"This bitch got me fucked up. Tico, this hoe just took my pussy lip. See if it's still there? I think my shit gone." She was staring at me with tears in her eyes, so I did what she asked.

"They still there and you can actually see em. You almost done, hang in there. You got this." When she started cursing again, I just turned my head and held her hand. Finally, we were done, and she was walking out limping.

"That's some bullshit. Women actually out here doing that shit? You niggas is not worth all that." Turning to face her, I looked her dead in the eyes.

"How you know? You might just need the right dick in yo life. That shit will have you doing all kinds of shit. No nigga gone wanna eat that shit with all that hair on it. Now, that bitch is pretty. You feel me." I could see her shaking when I licked my lips. I don't know why, but that shit had me turned on.

"Ain't no dick worth that kind of pain. I think I left my uterus on that bitch's table." This time, I laughed out loud. Dany looked at me and started laughing with me as she hit me in the arm. "That shit ain't funny. I think you did it on purpose because I had you and yo bitch fighting."

"Haven't you heard. I'm Mantico St. Lauren, Lil Mama. I ain't worried about shit out here. I damn sure ain't pressed over a bitch. We got in the car, and I drove her to Gucci. Grabbing some swimwear, shades, and slides I headed to the docks.

"I've ummm never been on a boat." Her ass was scared, and this was the first time she wasn't talking shit.

"I know Dany. You ain't been nowhere but to them raggedy ass courts." She started laughing and stopped mid laugh. I'm guessing, she finally noticed it.

"For Dany? Tico, you bought me a boat? Did you buy me a fucking boat?" Her fear went out the window then.

"Naw, Lil Mama. I named my yacht after you." I made sure I emphasized Yacht. Shorty was trying to downplay my shit and I wasn't having it.

"That is really sweet, Tico. For real, I love it. How do your bitch feel about you naming your yacht after another chick?"

"I've never brought another chick on here. I usually use it when I wanna get away from everything. It's my peace. Keep that in mind before you get on here with all your negative ass bullshit." Walking off, I climbed onboard before she could say anything. Dany didn't see a nigga was really trying to make things right, and her attitude was annoying as fuck.

No one would ever think to talk to me like she does because they knew I would dead they ass. Not Lil Mama. She tried me every chance she got. Going in the bags, I grabbed my trunks and shit and started taking off my clothes. As soon as I had my shorts pulled up, Dany finally figured out where I was and walked in the bedroom. Grabbing my sunglasses, I walked past her to head back upstairs.

"Put yo shit on and come on the deck. I'm about to have the chef whip something up." She opened her mouth again, but I kept it moving.

"Mr. St. Lauren, are we taking her out on the water today? Or are we just chilling."

"Take her out. Have the chef meet me on the deck." Going up to the second floor, I got on the chaise and laid back. Throwing my shades on, I stared out at the water.

"What can I get for you?"

"Get me a double shot of Anejo and make her an Amaretto Sour. Two steaks, medium well. Oh, add a couple of lobster tails on there with it."

"Any sides sir?"

"Loaded mash and roasted brussels sprouts." When they walked off, I continued to stare out at the water. Sometimes I couldn't believe I actually did it. I always said I was going to be that nigga, but to actually accomplish it was something most people never got the chance to do.

"I'm sorry if I've been an ass. I'm trying to readjust and shit just all off. I know you're trying to make things right, but I've been busting yo balls at every turn. I'm going to do better and chill out for these three days." Turning to look at her, I had to fight hard to maintain my expression. Dany was looking like she belonged on this bitch. Her body was flawless as fuck in her swimsuit and for the first time since I met her, I wanted to run my tongue over her entire body. The way her cover up flowed to the ground and the swimsuit fit every curve. Fuck, shorty was bad as hell.

"You act like you got a fucking choice. Sit yo thick ass down, you blocking my sun." I could tell she wanted to say something, but she sat on the chaise next to mine. The boat started moving and I could tell she was nervous. Her ass sat up and held the armrest on her chaise hard as fuck.

"Can we just stay on the docks?"

"Bring yo scary ass over here." I don't know what made her more nervous, me or the boat moving, but Lil Mama was shook. Grabbing her hand, I pulled her to me, and she didn't talk shit. Which was shocking. Lying next to me, Dany snuggled up close and comfortable. When her head laid against my chest, my hand automatically went to her waist. I don't know why, but the shit felt normal and right. She looked up at me and I could tell she wanted to say something, but nothing came out. I was about to go against everything I've been thinking and kiss her, when we were interrupted.

"I have your drinks." I'm glad I decided to go with the oversized chaise chairs when I decorated the yacht, because Dany was acting like she was on this bitch by herself. Sitting up, she grabbed her drink and passed me mine.

"Thank you, Harry."

"Your food will be up shortly." Nodding, I took a sip of my drink. I needed that mufucka after what almost happened. I don't know what I was thinking, but that wasn't the move. I was allowing Dany's sexy ass body to cloud my judgment and I needed to stop that shit.

"What is this called? It's so good."

"Amaretto Sour."

"This mufucka is fye." I watched her lips go around the straw and I could feel my dick bricking up. Knowing I needed a distraction, I decided to ask about something that wouldn't turn me on.

"So, tell me about your time in there. What was it like? Fill me in on what I missed." I briefly saw anger cross her face, but she changed her reaction.

"I mean, it was jail. You want me to ease your guilt and tell you I had it made? Well, I didn't. It was days I didn't eat because the food was inedible, and I didn't have commissary. When I first got there, some bitches tried to bully me, and I got sent to solitary for damn near killing her ass. You can barely get sleep because you don't feel safe. You never know if someone is going to come for you. Kema is the only person that visited me the entire time I was there, and no one wrote me." I wanted to tell her I wrote her letters, but I remained quiet.

"Shit was bad, but then I started to adjust. Before I knew it, I was a jail pro and I figured out how to survive. It wasn't easy, but I figured it out. I gave myself a goal in there. I had to focus on something for the time to fly by. So, I worked on my weight."

"I'm sorry. I know I keep saying the shit, but I really am. I hate that you made that decision that night, but I love you for it at the same time. I've never had someone I thought would have my back like that. Most people fear me, so they're scared not to. You, from the jump you was there for a nigga. That's what good friends do, and I wasn't a good friend back. I chose me over you and that shit wasn't cool. I know what I did was flaw, just know it wasn't my intent. I didn't know how to be there for you and for me at the same time."

"I get that. From the moment I took your gun, I knew what I was doing. They tried everything to get me to say your name, but I knew what I was sacrificing. I just didn't know I was losing you in the process. You may not know it, but you were the reason I survived."

"In jail?"

"No nigga. I wanted to kill your ass when I was in there. I'm talking about when my parents died. I saw you and fell in love. You gave me a reason to wake up every day. I went from being sad, to looking forward to something. I knew you didn't want me, but if I accepted that I would have no purpose. Now, I'm grown, and I have no idea what to do." Grabbing her by her face, I made her look at me.

"You live for you. Not me, not your parents, but for you. Figure out what you want and do that shit. The type of loyalty you have is rare. Just know, whatever you do out here you got me behind you. One hunnid."

"Thank you. Now, is there any food on this bitch. I'm starving." Shaking my head at her, I laughed hard as hell.

"I mean, you can eat this dick." When she hesitated, I let out a nervous laugh. I was dead ass serious, but the way that she started fumbling let me know that might not be a good move. "The chef bringing something up, Dany. Give it a minute."

"Okay." She leaned against me again and we laid there in silence just staring at the water, until the food came.

Even though I was scared to be out on that water, I didn't want to leave. It was so beautiful, and Tico did everything in his power to make sure I was comfortable. He kept staring at me and every time I thought he was going to make a move, I had to pick my face off the floor. The ambiance made it hard to keep my emotions in check, but I did it and we were now walking back to his car. As soon as we got inside, I laid my head back to take a nap. A bitch was tired, and I had at least an hour before we made it back to his house.

"Naw Lil Mama. Wake yo ass up. You not about to be snoring and slobbing in my shit." I looked into Tico's grey eyes and just wanted to stare into them forever. His tongue traced his thick ass lips and I swear I wanted to know what they felt like.

"What's on your mind?" He pulled off and I had to clear my throat to shake away the thoughts I was having.

"Nothing. I can't wait to get home. I'm tired as fuck. I'm not leaving that mufucka tomorrow. Oh, and you gotta go to the grocery store. I'm going to cook for you." His ass smiled when he glanced over at me, and I melted in my seat.

"I'm straight. You not about to be hooking me up no jail house meals and shit. I like real food Lil Mama."

"Shut the fuck up and just do what I asked."

"I'll get it done. I have a couple of meetings tomorrow, but I'll handle that first. You gone be good in the house by yourself?"

"I'm sure I'll find something to do. The house big enough. Maybe I'll throw a party or something." His smile faded and I knew I said something wrong.

"Never invite someone to my shit. I don't like people knowing where I lay. That will be the quickest way to get yo ass dead. Are we clear?"

"Yeah." Turning my head, I fought back the tears. This was one mean nigga, and it seems like every time I thought we were in a good space, something happened that had us arguing. I was over the shit, and I couldn't wait to get out his space. Closing my eyes, I ignored his ass until I felt the car stop. Looking around, we weren't at his house.

"Let's go." I had no idea where we were, but the house was beautiful. It was bigger than his and I swear he had a mufucka thinking about their life choices hanging out with him.

"Whose house is this? It's amazing."

"My parents." I was about to freak out, but it was too late. He was ringing the bell before I could protest. A butler opened the door, and I was impressed again.

"Hello Mantico. Welcome." I never knew that was his real name and I don't know why, but it turned me on. That shit was sexy as fuck.

"They're by the pool." Nodding, he walked off and I followed close behind him. I tried to look around, but he was moving too fast. We went through some patio doors and his parents were in the pool hugging. At least that's how it looked at first.

"Are they-..."

"What the fuck yall nasty asses doing?" They looked up shocked and started laughing.

"Maybe you should call first next time. Take your company in the tearoom. We will be in shortly. Your daddy almost finished." I could see the anger on Tico's face as he stormed off. I thought the shit was cute. Old love was always beautiful to see. It gave you hope that it's some relationships that could still last out here.

"They too old for that dumb ass shit. All the workers they got in the house, and they got they nasty asses out there fucking and shit." I giggled as he paced the floor.

"Mantico, it's okay. That's real love, so they don't care who knows it." He turned to face me, and my skin got hot from his deep glare.

"Say my name again." My ass was nervous, but I repeated it.

"Mantico."

"My shit sound sexy as fuck rolling off your lips." He was walking towards me, and my panties slowly began filling up with my juices.

"Son, is everything okay?" When he heard their voices, he stopped in his tracks. Walking over to this beautiful older lady, he hugged her.

"What up ma. I wanted yall to meet my friend, Dany." The guy that was standing with him turned to me quick as hell.

"Ahh, you're the reason my son is free today. Let me first say, thank you. I'm Manny, his father. This is Yvette, his mother." Walking over, I shook their hands nervously.

"It's nice to meet you both. If I had known I was coming here, I would have dressed more appropriately." His mother waved me off and grabbed my hand. Pulling me towards a couch, she sat down, and I did the same.

"You're fine. We've been dying to meet you. As soon as Mantico told us you were coming home, we insisted that he brought you over. Are you hungry sweetie?"

"No ma'am. We ate on the yacht." She smiled hard as hell.

"So, you've seen it. I loved the idea when he told me about it. I know what you did was a hard sacrifice but thank you. I hope my son is acting like he has some sense. Men tend to forget how to show their gratitude." I looked over at him and he was talking to his father watching me.

"He's trying. We can't seem to get along, but he is trying. I know it's my fault because I'm trying to put my feelings in their proper spaces, but it's hard you know? I hate him and love him at the same time. He left me in there, but now he acts as if I'm one of the most important people in his life." She placed her hand on top of mine and smiled.

"It's not your fault. He just doesn't like when you're angry at him. You have every right to feel the way that you do when it comes to him. His dumb ass just don't realize it's your love for him that is keeping you around. I take it you've met Celeste?" I found it strange as hell that she would tell me about his girlfriend when she didn't know me.

"Ummm."

"You're shocked that I mentioned her? I'm not one of those mother's that help their son cheat or get over. If his ass ain't been honest, that's on him. Either way, she won't last long. I know you may feel as if you don't have it in you to wait on him, but you will. I can see the look in your eyes, they mirrored mine. Just know, he's worth waiting for. Now, I'm not asking you to stop your life, but when the time comes, don't fight it."

"You waited for his dad?"

"Yeah, but my problem wasn't another woman. I had to wait on him to divorce the streets. I've always known he was more than that, he just had to realize it. Now, I'm waiting on my son to figure it out."

"What yall over here talking about? You better not be filling her head with bullshit; she already stays mad at a nigga."

"She gone see a nigga get his ass beat if he doesn't watch how he talk to me." They both laughed and it had me thinking about my parents. Manny must have noticed my demeanor change.

"Aight, We are going to have a dinner party this weekend. Make sure yall come by, but as of now, I need yall to get the fuck out. Me and my girl trying to finish some shit. You feel me," Manny said while looking at Yvette in a mannish way.

"That's my cue. We'll be there." Grabbing me around my waist, Tico led me outside back to the car. As soon as we got inside, I kicked my shoes off and got comfortable. Leaning over, I laid my head on his arm. I thought he was going to talk shit about me trying to fall asleep, but instead, he adjusted himself so I could get comfortable. Closing my eyes, I pretended I was laid in the bed cuddled up with him.

Mantico St. Lauren

Pulling up to the house, I looked down at Dany and she looked at peace. Reaching down, I rubbed the sweat beads off her nose and shook my head as she snored softly. You would think Lil Mama worked a job today the way she was acting. Pulling into the garage, I parked and tried to wake her up. Her ass didn't move, so I climbed out. Her head did a bounce since my shoulder was no longer there, but her ass continued to snore. Walking to her side, I opened her door and grabbed her out. Dany let out a moan, wrapped her arms around my neck, and continued to snore.

You would think someone who was in jail learned how to sleep light, but not her ass. Shaking my head, I headed inside and walked as fast as I could. Lil Mama looked good with her weight, but carrying her ass had a nigga's knees shaking. I started to throw her ass on the couch, but I said a silent prayer and headed up the stairs. It took me a while, but

I made it and was finally at her door. As soon as I opened it, she burst out laughing.

"For a minute there I thought you was going to drop me down the stairs." Realizing her ass played me, I dropped her on the floor. Let's see how funny she finds that shit.

"You petty as hell. A nigga got a bad back and you playing and shit. What if we would have fell?"

"I'm not that heavy mufucka. You could have at least carried me to the bed." Climbing off the floor, her ass laughed again, and I couldn't do shit but smile with her. "I'm going to get in the shower. If you not getting in with me, get out my room please." Lil Mama keep testing me she gone fuck around and get what she looking for. Rubbing my hand down my face, I walked out and went to my room. Yeah, her body was looking right, and I wouldn't mind sliding my dick inside her, but I wasn't trying to end up in a messy situation.

I was trying to get to know Dany and show her that a nigga wasn't flaw, but I didn't expect it to be this hard. When she went away, Lil Mama was slightly overweight, and looked homely as fuck. Not to mention her age. Milk had done a body good, and she was old enough to get dicked down. Removing my clothes, I went in the bathroom and jumped in the shower myself. As soon as I stepped in the water, my thoughts took over. When I met Celeste, a nigga had already made it. That was probably the reason I couldn't bring myself to love her. I always felt like when a nigga got on top, the best bitch to have by his side was a bitch that was there when he was struggling. It's something about coming up through the trenches with the love of your life. It's the relationship I always thought I would have since I started from the bottom and worked my way to the top.

Dany would have been perfect if she was of age back in the day. Lil Mama didn't hesitate to take the burner from me after making sure I got away safe. That's loyalty you could barely find in your niggas, let alone a bitch. They knew how to spend yo bread, but when the chips are low, mufuckas get ghost. Handling my hygiene, I climbed out and wrapped up with a towel. When I walked back in my room, Dany was in my bed under the cover.

"Let's watch a movie. I'm not sleepy and your house is too quiet and creepy." Shaking my head, I went in my drawer and grabbed some Polo briefs. Lil Mama was staring at me, so I dropped my towel right in her face and slid them on. Her mouth hit the floor and then she turned her head. Laughing, I climbed in the bed beside her, but I laid on top of the cover.

"Mantico, why you laying like that? You pulling the covers and shit." I knew she was testing me, but I played along. I needed to hide under them bitches anyway. The way she says my name had my dick bricking up. Pulling the covers, I slid under and grabbed the remote.

"All of a sudden, yo ass got a lot of energy. You was just in the car slobbing on my shoulder, now you wanna watch a movie. Fuck you want me to put on?"

"The shower woke me up. Put on an action movie, Mantico." This time, she rolled my name off her tongue, so I knew she was trying to fuck with me. Going to John Wick, I pressed play and tried to pay attention to the movie. Dany was making that hard to do because she was now laying on my chest while rubbing my stomach. I'm surprised my dick wasn't shaking her hand. That mufucka was jumping and I was ready to slide in some pussy. "So, what is this movie about? Is he a killer?

"Watch the fucking movie. If you stop doing everything else and watch the shit, you will see what it's about." I wasn't mad at her for rubbing on me, I was mad at me because I couldn't control myself.

"Okay sheesh. You mean as fuck for no reason. I was just trying to make conversation."

"Do you wanna talk or watch the movie?" When she didn't say anything else, I focused on the movie until I drifted off to sleep. I didn't even realize I was knocked out until I felt her mouth on my dick and not in a good way. Her teeth was scraping the fuck out my dick. "Hey, what the fuck you doing?" This mufucka had the nerve to look up and smile like she was doing something.

"I been wanting to do this for a long time. Just sit back and relax."

"How Sway. You got my dick meat in between yo teeth like the skin off some chicken. I'm good Lil Mama, let's just finish watching the movie." I could see the hurt on her face, but I wasn't trying to hurt her feelings. When the tears fell from her eyes, I felt like shit, but what was I supposed to do, let her take my dick off? Jumping up, she got out the bed and ran out of my room. I would have chased her ass, but I needed to tend to my dick. Ain't no telling how long she was down there. A nigga was probably missing about two inches fucking with shorty. Going to the bathroom, I looked over my meat and it was all types of scrapes and shit. Looking in the cabinet, I grabbed some Vaseline and prayed it didn't take long for my shit to heal.

She gave a new meaning to eating a dick. Wincing, I climbed in the bed trying to figure out how a nigga had injured dick at this age. Who didn't know how to suck dick in twenty twenty-one? I mean, even if yo shit was whack, you should know not to use your teeth and shit. Feeling like shit, I got up and walked to her room. Every time my dick rubbed against my briefs, that shit hurt, but I wanted to check on Lil Mama. Knocking on her door, I waited for her to answer, but she didn't. Opening it, I walked inside anyway.

"Hey, you good?"

"Tico, if you don't get yo rude ass out of my room, I'mma beat yo ass. How bout that. I don't know who the fuck you think I am, but you real close to getting these hands." I laughed trying to lighten the mood, but she wasn't going.

"I know I responded fucked up, but I wasn't expecting that. Dany, how the fuck you don't know how to suck dick? If you gone wake a nigga up, you gotta do that shit sexy. I know you always hungry, but you can't be trying to eat my shit for real."

"Fuck you. If you don't mind, I would like to go to sleep."

"Girl, you ain't that damn sleepy. I see them fucking cookies in yo bed. For real though, how you don't know how to suck dick?"

"Because I'm a virgin. I always wanted my first time to be with you but forget it." Walking over to her, I sat next to her on the bed.

"You save yo virginity for a nigga that deserve it. I ain't shit and you deserve better. Hearing you say nobody else been in that pussy got me ready to shift yo insides." Leaning in, I rubbed my hand between her legs. "But I have a bitch and that ain't fair to you. Dany, you're a real one and you need someone that's going to give you they all. I'm not him."

"I understand." Not wanting to hurt her anymore, I got up and walked out of her room. My dick was brick hard and I couldn't even jack the raggedy mufucka off. Shaking my head, I went in my room and climbed in the bed. Yeah, I had to hurry up and find her a place.

Danyelle Blakely

Waking up, I rubbed my temples. I had a headache out of this world. That nigga Tico basically said my head was whack, and that right there had me crying all muthafucking night. Getting up, I went in the bathroom and handled my hygiene. My nose got to twitching, so I knew it was some food being cooked somewhere in this bitch. No matter how mad I was, I wasn't turning down no food. Remembering that the last time I smelled food in here, it was Celeste I grabbed some booty shorts. I threw them on with a tank before heading downstairs.

This time, I found Tico at the stove looking confused and fucking some shit up. Shaking my head, I walked over to him and glanced in the pots. His ass was burning the hell out of some sausage, and his eggs was runny as hell. Pushing him out of the way, I turned the eyes off the stove and started grabbing more items.

"I guess I'm not the only one who don't know what the fuck they doing. Move, I got this." His ass scoffed and sat down at the island.

"Look, you're a virgin. How the fuck you think you supposed to know how to do it right? Of course you're going to fuck up. Bitches don't become head Gods because they seen some shit on a TV. A nigga gotta teach you and show you what he like. How the fuck you in here mad, but I'm the one in here with battered dick?"

"I know I probably wasn't doing it right, but you didn't have to be so fucked up about it." This time he laughed.

"So, what the fuck was I supposed to do? Keep letting you peel my skin off." That made sense but fuck that. He could have lied or said it nicely. The doorbell rang and his ass looked confused as he grabbed his gun and walked towards the door. My nerves kicked in, but this time I ducked in the corner in the kitchen. Ain't no way I was taking another case for him, so I was about to be Ray Charles in this bitch. I ain't heard nothing, and I ain't seen shit.

"Besssstttt. Where the fuck you at girl. Whew, you done fell the fuck off. Your cooking smell like burnt ass." Coming out into view, I ran to her and gave her a hug.

"Bitch, you know better. That nigga was in here trying to cook and fucked this shit all up." She started smiling hard as hell.

"Awww, he was trying to cook for you after you put it on him?" Tico laughed and walked out of the kitchen. Shaking my head, I started cleaning the pans, so I could get breakfast going for real. I looked around the corner to make sure he was out of earshot before I told her how it went down.

"So, yesterday we had this great day together. He took me on a Yacht, I went to meet his parents, and when we got home we were laid up watching a movie. When he fell asleep, I decided to go for mine like you always tell me. Bitch, I'm down there sucking his dick right, and that shit was too big to fit in my mouth, but I kept going. That nigga woke up and stopped me. Told me I was scraping his shit up. As if it couldn't get any worse, the nigga came in the room and basically told me I needed to find somebody else to fuck." I expected her to go off, but this bitch started laughing and was laughing hard as fuck too. She had tears rolling down her face, but I didn't find nothing funny.

"Best, please tell me you didn't shred that nigga's dick. I know you a virgin, but everybody know you don't use teeth. Lawd, I'mma have to teach yo ass a few tricks. I'm surprised he didn't beat yo ass."

"Fuck you. What you doing here anyway?"

"I just came to check on you before our meeting. You know this nigga swear he the fucking God father around this bitch. I figure, after the meeting we can go have a spa day or something."

"Okay, let me make these omelets real quick. You know a bitch starving."

"Me too. A bitch did a drive by on some dick this morning. That nigga Mink, whew I might have to cuff his ass." I tried to think back to where I heard that name.

"The dude from the club?"

"Yeah, it's Tico's right hand. His dick is heavy, and his pockets heavier. That nigga be paying out the ass for thirty minutes." I looked at her confused. Kema didn't have a nigga, so I had no idea why she was choosing to be a hoe.

"Friend, why you won't date him if he got it like that? I've seen him and he looks nice."

"Because I'm still weighing my options. He cool, but that's what's wrong with us bitches. Niggas will play the field until they know for a fact that chick the one. Bitches, we fall in love as soon as we get good dick. We cut everybody off and then look stupid when we find out he still entertaining. Won't be me." I continued to cook as I listened to her logic. Made sense to me. Hell, I fell in love with Tico way back then, and I hadn't even smelled the dick. I've never even looked at another guy.

"Don't be in here trying to build a hoe. You know her ass easily influenced and shit. Lil Mama, you a good girl and the right nigga gone treat you good. Don't listen to loose lips." Tico had walked in, and I guess he heard the conversation. He was fully dressed, and I had to admire how good he looked. Even though he was only in a Gucci cap, T shirt, and shorts, it always looked good how he wore it. Even his socks were Gucci.

"Best, you about to fuck that omelet up." Realizing I had zoned out, I took the skillet off the stove and put the first omelet on a plate. Passing it to Tico, I grabbed some orange juice out the fridge and poured him some. Kema was looking at me in disbelief.

"Damn Best. When did we start feeding niggas before each other? I been sitting here all this time and you gone give his ass a plate first. Give me a bite, Tico." He moved his plate away and dug in. Laughing, I went back to the stove to make her one.

"Girl, it's not gone take me long to do yours. You not out here starving no more. You should have let Mink take you out to breakfast." I knew I was being Messy, but that's what her ass gets talking shit.

"Why would Mink be taking you out to eat?" Kema started fumbling and I couldn't do shit but laugh.

"Because we fucking." She rolled her eyes at me hard.

"All I know is it better not intervene with my bread. You grown, and I can't tell you what to do with that hot ass pussy, but if he starts falling off or yall bring that drama to my shit, I'm shutting it the fuck down. Are we clear?" Realizing he was serious, I mouthed to Kema that I was sorry. This nigga was always angry and shit.

"I got it boss man. It's not like that. I fuck him, he pays me, and I leave."

"I'mma have to holla at my nigga. I taught him better than that shit. Mufucka out here paying for an overtly used 88 Buick. Lil Mama, this shit was fye as fuck. I'll be back in a few hours. Kema, get that shit to go. You know I don't do late. Let's get it."

"Throw my shit on a napkin and let's go. We gone have to share this mufucka."

"Tico, you can wait until I make my food. I'm going with yall. Me and Kema going on a spa day after yall meeting. For once, calm the fuck down." He stared at me with his grey eyes mad as hell, but then his look softened.

"You got it. Hurry up. My time is money." He walked out and I put Kema's omelet on a plate.

"Girl, I don't see how you deal with his shit. That's why I came over here to check on you. That nigga mean, and crazy as fuck. His girl been over here?"

"Not today. She can have his ass."

"That's what the fuck I'm talking about Best. We gone find you another nigga." I nodded and acted as if I agreed with her, but deep down I knew I was full of shit. It's only one nigga that ever had me gone, and his mean ass was waiting on me to finish cooking. Starting on my omelet, I thought about our day on the yacht and how perfect it went. It was moments like that, that had me stuck on his ass. I was going to ask him about my place today. Maybe I needed some space from him.

Mantico St. Lauren

"Aight listen up. We got a big shipment coming in tomorrow and I need all teams on point. Mink, you and your team need to be at the hanger at six am. Not a second after or don't bother coming back. Fil, I need you to make sure you and your team go to all the distros today and talk to them about new prices. Whoever good with it, they get the best fucking drugs to ever hit the streets. If they won't comply, dead they ass. No questions. Anyone you have to take out, make sure you get another crew to cover their territory.

Kema, go by the Saints and make sure the girls are ready to cut and bag this new shipment. If anybody in there slacking, call Mink and have him dead they ass. If my money is off, you already know. Is everyone clear on what they need to do?" When everyone nodded and didn't have any questions I moved on. "Good, let's get this bread. Only hit me up if you need me. If you can handle the shit yourselves, don't call me.

If you call me for some dumb shit, you already know how it's going."

Everyone started to pile out and I looked over at Dany. For some reason she looked disgusted. She had this expression on her face that had me trying to figure out what the problem was. I wasn't going to try long because I had too much going on to be worried about a bitch that wasn't mine. Lil Mama stayed in her feelings too much for me. I needed to be on point, so I didn't have time to pacify her feelings.

"Yo, Dany. We got a problem?"

"Nope boss man, it's your world. I'm just here waiting on my Best. You got it." She said that shit with so much attitude I couldn't do shit but shake my head. Before I could respond, Celeste walked in. The only reason she knew where the warehouse is, was because of my connect.

"Hey baby. I'm ready to go to lunch. Are you done here?" As soon as she said her last word, she looked over and saw Dany. "I see you and this bitch getting real cozy. You got the bitch on your roster now?" Dany and Kema jumped up and I knew I had to intervene.

"Take your ass outside and wait for me in the car. You always running yo big ass mouth and don't know shit. Make this yo last time you disrespect me or anybody in my shit." I could tell she was pissed, but she was getting out of hand.

"Wow. You talk a lot of shit but remember don't ever bite the hand that feeds you. Let this lil fat bitch send you off if you want to. I will have it real dry around this mufucka." Walking over towards her, I grabbed my gun and placed it at her head.

"You threatening me Celeste? You know how the fuck I feel about threats. When they made one connect, they made another. Don't get yo dumb ass dead trying to be something you ain't. Now, get the fuck out my shit. I'll talk to you later." She looked at me with tears in her eyes.

"Okay Mantico. I hear you loud and clear."

"What the fuck I tell you about calling me that shit. You still here and I'm trying to see why the fuck you still in my face." She walked out and I put my gun back in my waist. This shit was starting to be a problem and I didn't do problems.

"Whew, you told her boujie ass. That girl is extra as fuck. I don't see how you do it, but that's not my business." Dany laughed as she talked shit, but I wasn't in the joking mood. Grabbing one of the money counters that was lying on the table, I threw that bitch at her fast. If Lil Mama couldn't do shit else, her ass knew how to duck.

"ENOUGH! I'm not with the bullshit and I've been really trying not to fuck you up. I get you got a chip on yo shoulder, but if you keep trying to disrupt my shit, I'mma knock that bitch off. You feel me? I'm going to talk to a realtor now, hopefully I have you a place by the end of today. Go enjoy your spa day on me."

"Fuck you Mantico. I don't need shit from you. It amazes me how you think you can make up for what the fuck you did with some nail polish and a couch. YOU LEFT ME FOR DEAD WHILE I DID A BID FOR YOU!!! Do you understand that shit?" Walking across the room, I looked her dead in the eyes.

"Yeah, and do you understand that without me, you back to being a homeless bum with nothing? You going to jail is the best thing that could have happened to you. It guaranteed you will be taken care of for the rest of your fucking life." She had me heated, but as soon as the words left my mouth, I regretted it. Dany opened her mouth and then closed it back. The tears fell, but she didn't say a word. Her ass stormed out just like Celeste had.

"Damn, all yo pussy fed up. You must not be hitting that shit right. Bitches take anything when you giving them good dick." I looked at Mink and he threw his hands up in surrender.

"Naw, I don't pay for pussy. So, I tend to have real nigga problems."

"Touché bitch. Touché." Grabbing my phone, I called my realtor.

"I need a house or a condo by tonight. No matter what the cost, get this shit done."

"Well hello to you too, Mr. St Lauren. Is there a particular neighborhood you're looking for?"

"Yeah, close to me." I know I should have gotten her a spot way on the other side of town, but I knew I wasn't gone want to do that drive. I was still gone have to check on her ass, I just needed her out of my space.

"Give me a couple of hours. I think I have a condo about five minutes from your house that just went on the market. I'll text you over pics and the numbers and you can let me know if you want to see it."

"Say less." Hanging up, I laid my head back and closed my eyes. My life was perfect until Dany came home. I'm not blaming her, but I needed order. My peace is what keeps me on top. It's no room for mistakes, and I don't have to worry about that if I keep my shit in order.

****

I had an address, and the price was right, not that it mattered. I would pay anything for Lil Mama, she deserved it. Grabbing my keys, I went out to my car and climbed inside. Grabbing my phone, I sent Kema a text. Once she sent me an address, I drove that way. I knew I was gone have to deal with Dany's attitude, but maybe she would shut that shit up once she saw the place. Pulling up, I took a deep breath and went inside the nail place. Everyone was laughing at someone, and I walked closer to see what was going on.

"Please Dany. I'm sorry for everything."

"Miesha, I could have sworn I told you I would merk your bitch ass if I ever saw you near her again." She turned towards me, and I damn near threw up in my mouth. "But those drugs doing you worse I see. Get the fuck out before I forget you went against my order." That bitch was high as a kite and was damn near invisible. When Dany got locked up, I put her out her own shit and told her if I catch her raising anybody else's kid, or around my streets I was going to break my rule and kill her.

I haven't seen her since. I didn't live at the house, but me and my niggas made sure they ate and checked on them from time to time. I even fixed the place up. I eventually bought another house and got another guardian to look after the kids that remained. I still fund that shit and I go over and talk to the kids every now and then. I had to make sure the bitch wasn't putting on a front like Miesha's bitch ass.

"I'm sorry Tico. I needed money for some drugs, and I came over. I saw the girls and wanted to catch up. You think I can have a dollar?" Grabbing her by the neck, I dragged her ass out the door and turned to face Dany.

"You, let's go."

"I'm not done. My toes not even dry. Besides, I don't want to go with you. I'm good."

"Get the fuck up, and let's go before I remove your ass like Miesha." Jumping up, she stormed out the door towards me while Kema smirked at me.

"You want Best bad as fuck huh?"

"Shut the fuck up." Walking out, I went towards the car and got in. This crazy mufucka had her feet on my dash. "Have you lost your fucking mind? Do you know how much this car costs?"

"Obviously, more than I can afford. I told you my shit wasn't dry, but you insisted I came. So, drive. Your time is money right?" Not saying another word, I drove towards the condo. At this point, I didn't give a fuck if she didn't like it. Her ass was moving in that bitch. I tried my hardest to show her a nigga was fucking with her the long way, but if this how she wanted it, cool. I was going to give her the house, and the bread and be done with her ass. Fuck Dany!

"Hey, shorty. Why the fuck you running my business to mufuckas out here?" Rolling my eyes, I slid my feet under the fan trying to make them dry quicker.

"Mink, if you didn't want nobody to know you a trick, then stop tricking." I could hear him getting pissed, and I couldn't stop myself from laughing.

"I ain't no fucking trick, Kema. I like you, but I ain't about to keep playing this game with yo ass. I'm that nigga, and I ain't about to be chasing no bitch."

"Simmer down. You always acting emotional and shit. You know I don't think you a trick, but what we have works. You niggas say yall not looking for a bitch and yall supposed to be so damn hood. The minute yall get some good pussy and a chick with an ass, yall lose your fucking minds."

"Mannn, are you about to come suck my dick? I'm not trying to hear all that other bullshit." Smiling, I shook my head.

"I knew that's what you wanted. Next time, avoid all the crying and just say what you want. I'm going to have lunch and then I'll be over there right after. Have that dick clean and oiled up for me slick." He started laughing hard as hell.

"Aight, baby. Hurry the fuck up and it better not be with a nigga."

"I'll see you soon, big daddy." Hanging up, I paid the nail tech and walked out to my car. I was about to call Dany and ask her again to go with me, but my battery died. Looking around, I didn't bring my charger, so fuck it. I'm sure she was going to say no anyway. I know my Best would never understand, but Miesha was all I've ever known. My parents whoever the fuck they were threw me in a garbage can when I was one day old. I've always lied to everyone like I knew who my parents were and that they got hooked on drugs. Truth is, I've been tossed around from home to home like the trash my parents thought I was.

As fucked up as Miesha was, she kept me. Yeah, she was mean and all types of messed up, but who knows what happened to her along the way. She was the only constant in my life. Her and Danyelle. In a weird way, I've grown to love her in some form or another. I pulled up to the old house and thought about all the times we spent there. Yeah, it wasn't a perfect family, but we all bonded in one way or another. I even had some good times in that bitch. Now, it was rundown and looked abandoned. Getting out, I walked towards the door with an attitude. When I told Miesha I was coming, she said we would be having lunch. There was no way anyone was living in this house, so more than likely she sent me off.

Grabbing the knob, I went inside, and she was pacing the floor. When she looked up at me, a toothless smile spread across her face showing all her gums. I wanted to slap her ass for bringing me here, but I know she sick in the head. Reaching in my purse, I pulled out some money to give her.

"Hey baby, where is Danyelle. I needed her to be here. You have to go back and get her Kema." Now, I was confused.

She's never liked any of us too much, but she hated Dany the most.

"She's not coming. Look, I'm not about to eat in this rundown ass roach cot. So, take this money and think about using some of it to get a room or something. I know you a crackhead but have some dignity. Be one of them boujie mufuckas that hit the pipe in the closet when nobody looking. You around here looking like you done lost Isaiah and shit."

"Fuck you Kema." She snatched the money from me and I laughed. "You think you so smart, but now I got yo money and get to watch you get yo ass beat." I was about to ask her who and what army but thought about Ms. Pearly having Damon. I turned to look around, and sure as shit stank, some big burly ass nigga knocked my ass out. This foot loose teeth having mufucka set me up.

"Where is Dany?" Now, I was confused. What the fuck did they want with Best?

"I don't know. She left me at the nail shop. What is this about? Did Miesha promise you her in return for something?

She trying to pimp bitches now? Whatever it is, take me instead." My Best had been through enough and I refused to bring her one more piece of heartbreak.

"You are going to take me to her, or I'm going to kill yo dumb ass. Whose life is more important?" I thought about that long and hard. Of course, no one ever wanted to die. That was the dumbest question you could ever ask someone. I thought about the sacrifice my Best made for Tico and how much I respected what she did. I was hurt every day that I didn't have her, but that type of loyalty was rare. She never knew it, but I strived every day to be like her. Dany was the bravest, strongest, most loyal person I've ever known, and she was the only family I had.

"I don't know where she is. Who are you and why are you looking for her?"

"The nigga she was dancing on in the club, that was my baby brother. Her and that nigga gone die, and since you won't tell me where she is, you are too." Raising his gun, he pulled the trigger twice. My body flew backwards and Miesha scurried out of there fast like the roach she was. Whoever this nigga was, left out right behind her. His ass couldn't really be bout that life because he would have made sure I was dead.

Coughing up blood, I fought to pull myself up. It was hurting too bad, so I started crawling towards the door. With each motion, I wanted to die. My body was on fire, and I could feel myself dying. Knowing I needed to warn her, I shook my head.

"Bitch, you have to make it to her. You have to Kema. You can do this," I said out loud to myself. A pain shot through me, and I laid back down on the floor. I prayed someone came looking for me, but I knew that shit wasn't going to happen.

Danyelle Blakely

This nigga had me fucked up. He thought because he was the big man, everyone had to jump when he said jump. His smart mouth ass thought somebody was scared of him, but he had no idea how close I was to knocking his ass the fuck out today. It must be try Dany day, because this bitch Miesha walked in the door begging us to come see her sometimes. Hoe never wanted to cook for us before, but now she wanted to share a meal with us. The way she was looking, I'm sure she wanted us to provide that mufucka.

I tried to talk Kema out of it, but her slow ass said people deserved second chances, so she was going. I loved my Best, but sometimes that bitch was too caring for her own good. It was the same feature I loved about her. She was loyal as fuck and even though she talked big shit, she had a heart big as gold. If Tico hadn't come in, I probably would have let her talk me into going, just to get a good laugh. I didn't give a fuck about what Miesha wanted, and it would be funny as fuck to see she got what she deserved. Bitches like her loved preying on children and they usually get away with it. The state doesn't give a fuck about children in the system, so they don't check on them once they are gone. When one of the fucked up guardians fall on their ass, I can appreciate that kind of karma. I still never understood how this life shit worked. Bitches like Miesha was walking around living and given the chance to hurt someone else. Meanwhile, my parents were great people who cared and they're dead. Someone somewhere had a weird sense of humor.

"Let's go." Rolling my eyes, I climbed out of the car and looked up at the building in front of me. You could tell it was one of those expensive places because it had a doorman out front. I had no idea what we were doing here, but I was in awe. Tico didn't say a word, he just walked inside and went towards the elevator. Not knowing where I was, I followed behind him. Hitting the penthouse floor, he put in a pin, and I anxiously waited to see what was going on. When the elevator opened, we were inside of a beautiful condo. It was an open floor plan with high windows and ceilings. It was almost as if I could see all of Chicago from the window. I walked around in awe, but I was scared to touch anything that's how nice it was in there. The house was staged with white furniture and carpet.

"Should we take our shoes off?" Tico looked at me and laughed.

"Mina, I'm here." Some gorgeous ass woman walked in with a tight skirt, see through blouse, and the highest heels I've ever seen.

"Hey, St Lauren. You could have showed her around. You didn't have to wait for me." She leaned in and kissed him on the cheek making me slightly jealous.

"I'm Danyelle." Bitch wasn't about to act as if I wasn't in the room. Hoe was going to acknowledge me, or I was going to make her see me.

"Oh, I'm sorry. Excuse my manners. I'm Mina. Let's show you around and hopefully this will be your home by the end of the day." My eyes damn near popped out of my head. I looked towards Tico, and he just walked off and started looking around. Since this was going to be my place, I did the same. I already knew I was in love, and I was going to say yes, I just wanted to see the rest. The kitchen was huge, it was three bedrooms and each one had a bathroom inside. The walk-in closet was damn near the size of another room. I didn't have that many clothes, but I couldn't wait to fill it with something. Walking back to the front, I stood off to the side as they laughed and joked about something.

"Danyelle, do you like it?"

"I love it. I can't wait to decorate it and make it mine."

"Okay, St Lauren they're asking five hundred. Is that too much or do you want to try and negotiate?" I waited nervously for his respond.

"She wants it, doesn't matter the price. Give her the keys and I'll wire you over the money." He went to walk out, but I stopped him.

"Mantico, can I talk to you for a minute." He looked annoyed, but he followed me to the master bedroom. As soon as he walked inside, I closed the door. I don't know what came over me, but I ran towards him and jumped around his waist. "Thank you so much. I absolutely love it." Not thinking, I placed kisses all over his face. The last one landed on his lip causing me to pull back nervously. He stared at me intently before his mouth covered mine. I've never kissed a guy before, so I was nervous and trying not to fuck it up.

"St Lauren, I'm going to head out. I'll be back with the paperwork." He groaned, so I knew our moment had passed. Climbing down slowly, I looked at him nervously waiting on him to hurt my feelings.

"Aight. Hit my phone." When he turned to look at me, I held my breath. "Let's go." I'm sure my disappointment was written on my face.

"Okay." His hand went around my waist, as he led me out the room.

"If I'm going to fuck you, I would rather it be in my own shit. I don't know who the fuck laid in them beds." Hearing him say that had my pussy jumping and ready. I had no idea how far we were from his house, but I prayed he didn't change his mind. When we pulled up five minutes later, I was excited. I practically jumped out the car and ran to the house. Surprisingly, he was right behind me. I had no idea where we should do it, but I went to his room and immediately started removing my clothes. As soon as he walked in the door, his eyes locked on mine and never wavered. Lying on the bed, I shook nervously as I kept my eyes trained on him as well. It seemed as if he was walking in slow motion towards me, causing me to nervously await his touch. This nigga's body was flawless, and I had no idea what was going to happen next. He came to me until we were face to face.

"Dany." I have no idea why he was whispering, but I responded in the same tone.

"Yes, Mantico."

"You're a virgin, and I ain't shit. This can't happen again, and I know how you feel about me. You sure you want to give me this pussy?" It didn't even take me a second to think it over.

"Yes. It was always for you." This nigga closed his eyes and when they opened up again, I knew he was on demon time. Without warning, he grabbed my legs and pushed them behind my head hard and fast. Before I could say nigga hold on, I'm a lil big I'm not that flexible; his mouth was on my pussy. I've imagined what this felt like a million times, but I wasn't ready. His tongue was circling my shit and then his shit went in high speed flicking fast as fuck.

"Ohhh fuck. Shit. Oh my God. Yeah, yeah, yeah!" I had no idea what the sex verbiage was supposed to be, but I'm sure my ass was out here sounding like one of them old hoes off the porn tapes from the seventies. It was the only guidance I had when it came to sex.

"Aww hell naw. You in here sounding like one of them annoying white women. If you don't say suck this pussy or something, I'mma stop." Giggling, I decided not to say anything at all. I was gone have to ask Kema what I supposed to say. My body started to shake, and I could no longer contain my screams. His tongue was deadly, and I just knew I was about to have a seizure or something. When he climbed up, I thought we was done, but the look in his eyes told me I was wrong. Leaning over me, he kissed me allowing me to taste my juices. "That pussy good ain't it?"

I just nodded, so I wouldn't embarrass myself any further. He kissed me for about five minutes straight and I couldn't believe this shit was happening. Everybody thought I was full of shit when I kept saying he was going to be my first, but here I was.

"Lil Mama, this gone hurt."

"Wait, what?" His response was a hard thrust into my pussy. I thought the nigga was going to take his time and slide it in slowly, but he decided to go with the shock factor. He screamed out hard, and I'm sure his dick was probably hurting from the teeth marks I put on him. My pain matched his, so I was screaming out with him. It wasn't until the pain was gone, that he slowed up his pace. I had no idea what to do, so I just laid there holding him tightly around the neck. When he pulled away, I thought I did something wrong, and he was about to stop. Instead, he spread my legs as if he was trying to put them in a Chinese split.

Pushing down on my legs, he went deeper inside of me as if that big ass dick could go any further. I knew if I said anything my ass was going to stutter and sound dumb. The only noise in the room was from the sounds of my pussy juice and his occasional groans.

"Fuck, how I'mma let this pussy go Dany?" I didn't know what to say, so I remained quiet. "You better not give another nigga my pussy." I got excited because I assumed that meant he was going to leave Celeste alone. We fucked, so we go together now.

"I promise I won't." As soon as those words left my mouth, his pace increased, and he started slamming in my pussy like he was trying to push my shit up to my neck.

"Fuck, I'm about to cum." His body jerked and next thing I knew he was rolling over. I laid there looking goofy with a smile on my face even though my pussy felt like it was on the floor. His ringing phone brought me out of my happy place.

"What's up Celeste?" I looked at him like he was crazy. How the fuck was he going to answer her call right after we fucked? "Slow down. What happened? Who the fuck shot up my warehouse and how do you know?" I was trying to eavesdrop, but I couldn't hear her side of the conversation. "I'm on the way." Hanging up, he got out the bed and went in the bathroom. I sat there looking stupid because I didn't know what to say. When he came back in the room, he immediately threw his clothes on getting ready to leave.

"Can you let someone else handle it? If they just shot it up, it's not safe for you to go. Is it?" He looked at me like I was crazy.

"You know what type of nigga I am. That's my shit, so I need to find out what happened. I'll be back."

"How am I going to call you and check on you?"

"Damn, I forgot you don't have a phone. Here, this is my phone. I only use this to call my connect, so don't use it unless it's an emergency. I'll get you one later or tomorrow." He put his number in the phone and just like that, he was gone. No kiss, no goodbye. Nothing. Not wanting it to ruin my moment, I limped to his shower and got in. I needed to put some hot water to this pussy. My shit was thumping, and it wasn't a great feeling, but I knew it would get better once I got used to his size. Smiling, I thought about what happened as the water soothed my shit.

An hour later, I was climbing out and it felt a lil better. Walking to my room, I grabbed some shorts to put on and a tank. Wanting to feel close to him, I went back to his room. As soon as I got comfortable in the bed and found something to watch on tv, his doorbell sounded off. I had no idea who it could be, but I went to go answer it. Tico never gave me instructions on what to do if someone just showed up, so I said fuck it. Maybe it was Celeste. If it was her, I was gone make sure she knew I just took that nigga from her. Opening the door, I wasn't prepared for the sight in front of me.

Screaming, I dropped to the ground and almost passed out

from all the blood.

Mantico St. Lauren

I could see the look on Dany's face when I answered Celeste's call, but I thought I was clear on where we stood. I guess it's true what they say, women hear what the fuck they want to hear. I knew I was going to have to deal with that when I got back to the house, but right now I had bigger problems. My main concern was finding out who was bold enough to shoot up my warehouse, and secondly why the fuck was Celeste popping up at my shit?

She knew I didn't play those type of games, but she thought she was exempt because of her ties to the connect. I see now I was gone have to make myself a lil more clear or Celeste was gone become a problem I had to handle. When I pulled up, nothing looked out of order, so I was a little bit confused. Grabbing my gun, I stepped out of my car and eased inside. Everyone was sitting around like nothing happened. Sitting down in front of them, I laid my gun on the table. I wanted to incite fear before I spoke.

"Hey nigga, why the fuck you come in here like Ike when he laid the gun on the table. You see Anna Mae was bothered, that shit don't work." I gave Mink a look to shut the fuck up. He was my right hand, but this was not the time.

"I have a few questions." I waited until I had everyone's attention before I spoke again. Seeing it was some new niggas in my shit, I turned my attention towards them. My business was like my house, mufuckas knew I didn't like people I didn't know in my shit.

"Was my warehouse shot up today?"

"Man, I don't know what the fuck that was. We was in here, some shots rang out, but nobody or nothing was hit." Fil spoke up as I pointed my gun at one of the new niggas and pulled the trigger.

"My bitch was here when they start shooting and I find you mufuckas in here kicked back instead of painting the mutha fucking city." I raised my voice on the last part and they were starting to see where they had fucked up at.

"Nothing was hit, so we don't even know if they was shooting at us. We just heard gunshots. When we went outside, Celeste was ducking down, but nobody was out there." I'm guessing Fil was their spoke person because he was the only one trying to explain. Pointing my gun at the next nigga, I pulled the trigger.

"Hey Foe, what you on?" Mink stood up with his hands in surrender, but I wasn't trying to hear none of that shit.

"Is there another building around this bitch? Who the fuck was they shooting at if they wasn't shooting at us? More importantly, why the fuck did I get a call from her, but not none of you niggas?"

"Shid, they could have been shooting at her for all we know. She said she was good, got up, and left. Nothing seemed out of order, so we didn't wanna bother you." This time, I pointed my gun at Fil.

"If they shooting at my bitch, they shooting at me. Anybody under my umbrella gets the same protection as me. Do you have a problem with that shit my nigga?" Mink walked over and stood in front of him trying to calm me down.

"Hey bro, you going too far. I get why you mad, but we will figure out what the fuck is going on. Fil, call it in and have somebody clean this shit up. The rest of you niggas, hit the streets and figure out what the fuck is going on. A couple of yall follow Celeste. Don't be obvious, just make sure she good until we can figure out what's happening." Everyone started moving out, so I lowered my gun. Fil was still looking at me shocked, so I turned my attention back to him.

"We got a problem?"

"Naw, but it seems like you trying to make it one. I get why you mad, I was just trying to explain what happened. We fucked up, but that don't mean you gotta son me like that in front of niggas."

"Who the fuck was them lil niggas anyway? Yall know I don't do new people in my space."

"Shid, you asked us to expand if mufuckas wasn't complying, so that's what we did. You just took out the mufuckas that was supposed to run their territory." It was no way I was going to admit to my mistake, so I just nodded.

"Aight, find some more niggas that's loyal and ready to make bread. Don't bring em here until they are fully vetted. I want everybody in their family checked out all the way down to the baby that just came out their girl's pussy." Fil started making calls and I felt bad. He's been my nigga from the beginning, but I couldn't tolerate stupid shit. My phone started ringing, and it was Celeste.

"Is everyone okay? I couldn't stick around to see, I had to get out of there." For some reason, her saying that had me thinking about Dany. It was no way she would have left. Shorty would have either tried to shoot back or at least made sure they was good.

"Yeah, they said it was only shots outside. You made it seem like mufuckas shot my shit up."

"Well, how was I supposed to know? I heard shots and I got out of the way. Of course, I had to tell Julio. Just in case it had something to do with his product." If she was in my face, I would have choked piss out her asshole.

"You overstepping, and I promise I'm about to knock yo ass back over that line. You don't show up to my warehouse unless I ask you to. You don't call Julio unless I ask you to. Bitch, I'm two seconds from telling you not to breathe, unless I ask you to." I could practically hear her blowing me off through the phone.

"You keep talking like you're putting me in my place, but you seem to keep forgetting, I have none. I'm that bitch Tico. I love you, and it seems like this lil hood rat is clouding your judgment. We've never had these problems before her." I agreed with that shit. Not that I was being influenced by Dany, but Celeste was intimidated by her.

"Take a minute and think shit over. I want you to play with something safe, Celeste. I really do, but if you're determined to keep crossing that line, I don't mind knocking yo shit back. Stay the fuck out of my business with Julio, or we're going to have a problem. I'm not into repeating myself, so please don't make me do it again." Not waiting on her to respond, I hung up. I was going to fall back off her for a second. She needed time to remember who the fuck I was. The only reason she got this many chances was because of my rule. I really hated doing kids and women, but she was pushing a nigga. Not to mention, I did care about her. Shit was good until Dany came home. The moment she saw her, everything went to shit. Seeing everything was being handled, I could get back to Dany. I know she was expecting me to make love to her, but I knew it would have hurt her more if I took my time. That shit was good as fuck, and I owed it to her to at least give her the experience she's dreamed about all her life.

"Hey Fil, my bad nigga. We good?"

"Yeah, we good. Shid, with a bitch like Celeste, I can see why you're stressed the fuck out." I laughed and walked outside. My phone rang, but before I could answer it, shots rang out.

Running in the house, I looked around for a piece of mail. Hell, anything with Tico's address on it. I couldn't find shit, so I ran frantically from room to room snatching shit out. My hands were shaking, and I was getting blood everywhere. I finally made it to his room and searched high and low. Seeing a file cabinet, I pulled it out and found some mail. One was paperwork on Tico's house, but the rest were letters addressed to me.

I didn't have time to figure out what the fuck was going on with that, so I threw them back inside, grabbed the phone he gave me, and took off down the stairs. I needed his address to call 911, and now I had it. My hand was shaking so bad, I could barely dial those three numbers. Sitting on the ground, I tried to stop the bleeding, but that shit wasn't working.

"Hello, I need an ambulance. My sister was shot. I have no idea who shot her, she showed up like this. Please, come help her." I gave them the address and hung up the phone. Dialing Tico, I cried hard as I waited for him to answer. When he didn't pick up, I dialed him again. When he didn't answer, I threw the phone down and picked Kema up in my arms. She was coughing up so much blood, I couldn't do shit but rub her hair and cry.

"I got you Best. Just like you've always had me. I promise, I got you. Just hang on, they on the way." She kept trying to say something to me, but I couldn't make out her words. She was choking too hard. "Don't try to talk, it's okay. I got you friend. You can't die on me. Not today. You're all I have Kema, and I refuse to let you go."

"My, my, myyyy." She was insisting on telling me what she had to say.

"Your what Best? Your parents? You want me to call your parents? I don't know what you're trying to say. Please, don't do this to me. I need you so much."

"My-..." She started coughing so hard that time, blood flew in my face. Using my shirt, I wiped her mouth.

"It's okay, Kema. Whoever you want me to tell something to, you can tell them yourself. You're going to be here to let them know. Just hang on a little while longer." Leaning back, I grabbed my phone and dialed 911 back.

"911 what's your emergency?"

"Bitch, I already told you what was wrong. Why the fuck they still not here yet? I need them to hurry. Please tell them to hurry."

"Ma'am, someone is on the way. Is the person still conscience?" Hanging up, I didn't bother to answer her question. Kema reached out her hand to me and grabbed mine. When she squeezed hard, I knew she was trying to tell me she loved me.

"I love you too, Best. Always. I know you're tired. I can hear your breathing slowing. It's okay, you can go to sleep now. I don't know what I'm going to do without you, but don't worry about me. Close your eyes and go to sleep, Best." Kema nodded her head and closed her eyes. She continued to squeeze my hand as her breathing shallowed. I sat there holding her until she took her last breath.

I could finally hear the sirens in the distance, but it was too late. The only person in the world that loved me was gone. Holding her as tight as I could, I broke down and cried real tears for the first time since my parents died. I had no idea what I did or what type of black cloud I had over me, but everything I love leaves me. If I hadn't asked my parents to go on the fourth, they would still be alive. If I had never left with Tico, Kema would still be alive. Realizing I was the common denominator, I knew I had to get away from Tico. He was the last person on this Earth that I loved.

"Ma'am, can you let her go. We need to check her. Ma'am, we need you to let her go." Leaning down, I kissed my Best on her cheek and let her go. Standing up, I left my entire heart lying on the porch as I cried hard. The pain was unbearable. "Ma'am, are you okay? Ma'am." I tried to take a step when my body dropped to the ground.

****

Lying in the hospital bed, I couldn't do anything but cry. The police had come in and officially pronounced Kema dead. She was the only person that chose to have my back. Yeah, my parents did, but they were supposed to. It was their job. Yeah, they were the best parents anyone could ask for, but they loved me because they were mine. Kema, chose to make me her family. She chose to look after me and make sure I was okay. It was nothing forcing her to bond with me, but she did. It was days Miesha only wanted to take me to the basement, but Kema always came with me. She never let me endure that shit by myself. Even when I took the case for Tico, he didn't stick by me. Kema was there every step of the way.

"Where the fuck is she? You better get the fuck out of my way or I'll burn this bitch to the ground." You could hear Tico screaming, but I wasn't impressed. I called him today when I needed him, and just like last time, he wasn't there.

"Sir, she is still in shock. We need her to rest. If you can come back tomorrow, that will be better for her. We gave her some medicine to sedate her." I heard the lady scream and then I could feel him standing close to me.

"Dany, what happened? I came home and it was blood all over the porch. The neighbors said someone had died. I thought-... I thought you were gone." Lifting my gown, he looked me over trying to see what was wrong with me. When he was convinced nothing was wrong with me, he climbed in the bed and pulled me close to him. "Dany, what happened?"

"Kema. Somebody killed her. The doorbell rang and when I opened the door, she was lying there bleeding. They took her from me."

"Who? Did she say who shot her?"

"No, she just kept saying her something. All I heard was my. She died in my arms, Tico." He grabbed me and held me tight, but I didn't want him to touch me.

"I know these hurts, and the last thing you want to hear are promises. It's nothing that is going to bring your friend back, but I am going to send her some company. I'm going to have the crew on this night and day until we figure it out. As soon as I get word on who it was, I'm going to deaden they ass myself."

"Who would do something like that to her? She didn't deserve that, and I can't help but wonder if this would have happened to her if she wasn't working for you. Did you know I called you?" The look on his face let me know he saw where the conversation was going. His jaw was jumping, but he tried to keep a sympathetic look on his face.

"Dany, don't do that. Kema made her decisions and I've always taken care of her. Anyone getting in this life know the risks." I couldn't believe he was saying this shit to me right now.

"Tico, I don't think I need to be your friend anymore. When they release me, I'm going to get my stuff out of your house, and we can go our separate ways."

"I know you're angry right now, but I'm not leaving you. Not this time. I got you Lil Mama. Just let me show you."

All I heard were more bullshit promises. Closing my eyes, I pretended to go to sleep. I hope that would get him to leave, but it really didn't matter. Not able to control the tears, I laid there with my eyes closed.

Mantico St. Lauren

On the outside, I was cool, but when I saw all that blood a nigga was losing it. After all the crazy shit that happened today, I didn't know what to expect. When I was leaving out the warehouse, a mufucka drove by and shot at me and I been on ten ever since. The only reason I came to the house was to change and get my arsenal of guns. We were about to have a black out, and I needed my shit.

It fucked me up to find out it was Kema, but I ain't gone lie, I was glad it wasn't Dany. I feel like I still haven't been able to make things right. Every time we took one step forward she knocked my ass back. Just like now, I was trying to be here for her, but I get the feeling she doesn't want to be bothered. It was no way I was leaving her, but I did need to step out and make a call. Mink had no idea what happened, and I had to break it to him.

"You hungry or you need anything, Lil Mama? I need to step out for a minute, but I'll be close."

"I'm okay." She turned her back on me, but I still leaned down and kissed her on the back of her head. I've never lost anyone close to me, so I had no idea how she felt. The closest I ever came to losing someone was when she went to jail.

"Aight, I'll be back. Call me if you change your mind."

"Why? I'm sure you won't answer," she mumbled it, but I heard her loud and clear. Knowing I had bigger shit to deal with, I chose to ignore it. Pulling my phone out, I called Mink.

"What up, nigga? You late. The entire crew waiting on yo ass, so we can go handle this business."

"That has to wait. Meet me at the hospital down the street from my house. We still having a black out, but we about to turn this bitch midnight."

"Aww fuck. I'm on the way." I'm sure he thought it was something dealing with me, but this wasn't the type of news you tell someone over the phone. I had no idea how deep they had gotten, but Mink was a good dude. The fact that he was sneaking around with her let me know he liked her. All the other chicks he fucked with, he hit they ass a couple of times and sent them on their way. He thought I would have a problem with it, so he snuck around and hid it from me. Knowing I had an hour before he got here, I jumped on the elevator and went down to my car. I've been here for hours, and a nigga needed something to eat. Not wanting to go far, I swung by The BBQ Patio and grabbed me a half white and fries. Even though Dany said she wasn't hungry, I grabbed her one too.

Not wanting to talk about it in front of Lil Mama, I sat in the car and waited for Mink to get to the hospital. Grabbing my food out the bag, I started fucking my food up. The shit was good as hell and that was the best thing about Chicago. It was a lot of bullshit, but the food was the best hands down. My car door opened, and Mink slid in.

"How you know where I was?"

"You can't miss that big ass head bitch. Now, quit stalling. What's up?" Closing my food up, I sat it to the side and thought about how I could say this shit. I wasn't trying to drag it out, but I wasn't trying to gut punch him with it either.

"Aight, look. When I got back to the house something happened. Dany said Kema showed up and she was shot. I'm sorry, bro. She didn't make it." He looked at me and started laughing.

"Aight, for real what's up? I know you don't want me fucking with shorty, but it's good. It won't interfere with the business. I know she good because I talked to her. We meeting up when she done handling business." I could see his expression change once I gave him a sympathetic look. "Bro, we meeting up after she done." His tone sounded like a plea. As if he could wish it true. Grabbing his phone, he dialed her number. It went straight to voicemail. He dialed her about four times before he sank in the seat.

"I'm sorry, bro. We gone find out who did this shit. I promise you."

"I know you need to get back upstairs to your girl. Tell her to hit me up and let me know when the services are. I know you said we're going to find out who did it, but I'mma go get started." Mink didn't say anything else, he got out the car and left. Knowing I couldn't let my nigga go out there by himself, I headed upstairs. This was my fucking city and if anybody was going to make this mufucka bleed, it was going to be me. Getting off the elevator, I headed to the nurse's station.

"Hey, discharge Danyelle Blakely."

"Sir, I don't think she's ready for that. We still have been giving her meds to sedate her. She's been quite out of it."

"Did that sound like a request? Discharge her or everyone in this bitch gone need a new place to lay their head. You feeling me?"

"I'm discharging her now." Walking in her room, I decided to take a different approach.

"Hey, Lil Mama. They letting you out of here. I know you was ready to go to the condo, and I'll take you as soon as I get back. Me and Mink about to hit these streets to find out what happened. When I get back, I'll drop you off." She didn't say anything, but she stood up and grabbed her clothes. As soon as she finished getting dressed, the nurse walked in with her papers. Placing my arm around her waist, I guided her out the door. I wasn't surprised when she pushed my shit away and walked towards the elevator.

The ride back to my house was silent, but at least it was quick. Not wanting her to see the blood, I made sure I pulled in through the garage. Lil Mama didn't say shit, she just got out and went inside. Walking in the door, I grabbed my gun out and did a walk through. With all that was going on, I needed to make sure no one was inside. Once I made sure everything was good, I went to her room.

"Aight, I'm out. I'll put your food on the counter if you get hungry." Not waiting for her to respond, since I knew she wouldn't, I walked out and headed to my basement. Grabbing my phone, I called Fil.

"Hey, put some niggas on my crib. They don't need to go inside, and they don't need to be seen. Let them know if a hair is moved on Lil Mama's head, I'm going after anyone they know."

"Say less. You want me to put someone on Celeste too?"

"Nigga, they should still be tailing her since earlier. I'm sure she good though. Where Mink at?"

"Nigga out here beating the shit out of somebody for answers. I have no idea how he chose where to start, but it seems like my nigga unhinged."

"Aight, send me your location and don't leave. No matter what that nigga says. I'm on the way." Grabbing two desert eagles, an AR, and my favorite bitches Beretta, I headed to my car. Looking at my phone, I saw the location and headed that way. It took me a little under an hour, but Fil texted and told me Mink was heading to one of the traps in the city that like to use bitches to stick up niggas, so that's where I pulled up. Grabbing my eagles, I got out the car. Mink was on his way in the door when I stopped him.

"I'm with you nigga. You ready?" he looked up at me and my nigga looked broken as fuck.

"It's about to be a black out."

Danyelle Blakely

Looking around, I had no idea what to do. My heart was hurting so bad, and I had no idea how to stop it. I knew I had to figure out a way to find her parents, but I had no idea where to start. Either way, my girl was going to have a great service even if I was the only mufucka in that bitch. I had no idea when Tico was going to come to take me home, so I went downstairs to get my food.

A bitch didn't want to tell him I was hungry, so I ignored him. My stomach wanted to slap the shit out of me, but I held out. Now that he was gone, I was about to tear that shit up. Putting it in the microwave, I fought doing a dance. Normally, Kema would be asking for half and that shit only made my heart hurt more. Pulling it out the microwave, I sat there and stared at it for a while before I finally decided to take a bite. Each one I took, another tear fell.

I had so many food stories with my bitch, I would never be able to eat without thinking about her. She was so hungry, every time she came to visit me, she would ask about the food I ate in the penitentiary. Kema's ass would go home and try to make the food I ate, and the next time she visited me, she would tell me how she liked it. I really don't think she gave a fuck about that food, but it was her way of staying connected to me. My Best always wanted us to do everything together, including jail. Thinking about jail made me remember the letters, grabbing my food and a soda, I took off running.

I don't know why I looked around first, but I did before I entered Tico's room. Sitting my food down, I went to his file cabinet and pulled out the stack of letters I saw with my name on it. Seeing the blood, froze me in my tracks. Trying my best to shake it off, I walked over to the bed and got comfortable in the middle. Looking at the post dates, I found the first one and opened it as I started on my chicken.

What up Lil Mama.

I'm not gone ask you how you doing because I'm sure the shit is fucked up in there. I went by the courts and the shit don't seem the same with you not standing on the sidelines watching me. I remember that night we was talking and you said I saved you. How you got up every day looking for me to make your day go by. I never told you or anyone else this, but I looked forward to you always coming up to me talking. Everyone in my circle fucked with me because they had to. No one gave a fuck what was on a nigga's mind or what I went through. Not you though. Yo ass checked on me every day and a nigga looked forward to that. It wasn't until I no longer had you, that I realized how much I needed you. Dany, you were my normal in a harsh cruel world. You believed in me so much that you gave yo life up for me. I know you can't see it, but I'm going to make it. For you. I'm going to be to you what you were to me. You won't understand why I haven't been to see you, and I will lie and say it's for the business. Truth is, I can't deal with the guilt. Knowing I'm the reason you were taken away from me. I'm fucked up, I know. Just know your sacrifice won't be in vain. You're special to me, always have been. I'm sorry I waited until it was too late to tell you. I won't make that mistake again and

I promise when you come home, I'll take every day to show you. I know you will want to see my face, but you know how a nigga look. I may not be there in the physical, but I promise to write you every day that you're there. Keep yo head up and don't let them bitches steal yo pussy. Tuck and duck. Lol just playing. See you same time tomorrow Lil Mama. -Tico

I don't know why, but reading his letter had me crying. All this time, I thought he didn't care. Like he was giving me a pity thank your or some shit. It was bigger than that and now, I wanted to know more. Seeing him say he wrote me every day, there was no way he could have. Jumping up, I ran over to the file cabinet and opened the other drawers. Sure enough, they were all packed with letters to me. Grabbing them all, I went to the bed and started reading.

Everything that I missed out on, from his come up to bitches that pissed him off. Even when he met Celeste. Tico told me every single detail of his life. It felt like I was there with him. I laughed and cried reading through the letters. I was happy he included me, but it hurt to know everything I had missed out on. Through his letters, we became best friends. I'm sure it was no one else he told some of the shit he told me. Even though I never saw them when I was in there, I'm reading them now. Tico told me the most intimate details of his life. Wiping my eyes, I laid back on his bed. I had a mixture of happy and sad tears rolling down my face. I was wishing Kema was here, so I could tell her everything. I knew she was somewhere smiling down on me saying suck his dick good Best. I laughed so hard, I started crying. Hard. I wanted me Best. I needed her, and she was gone. The pain became unbearable, and all I could do was close my eyes and go to sleep.

****

Feeling kisses on my face, I opened my eyes and Tico's grey eyes were staring back at me. I had no idea what to say, so I just stared at him. Leaning down, he kissed me again but this time with passion.

"I'm sorry, for everything." Before I could say anything else, he started removing my clothes. Our eyes never left each other's. Tico was being gentle, and he had my body shaking. Trailing his finger from my neck to my stomach, he had my mind distracted. It was what I needed at the moment.

"Mantico." Covering my mouth with his, he silenced me.

"You don't have to say anything Lil Mama. It's all on me and I'm going to fix it. I know it seems like I don't do shit but let you down, but a nigga trying. I just wanna make shit right." I could feel his dick at my opening and this time, he slid in slowly. Each stroke had me remembering why I was in love in the first place.

The tears slowly fell, as I grew more in love. I had no idea what the fuck was going to happen after this, and I wasn't ready to say goodbye to my Best, but for now, the moment was perfect. It was no pain, and my pussy was leaking fire and water at the same damn time. My body started shaking and I knew I was about to experience some shit that was going to activate my crazy.

"Fuck Lil Mama. I'm about to cum." I had an orgasm, and I could feel his body shake after me. He rolled over and stared at me. "Hey, I see you been looking through my shit. Can you put these mufuckas up now, I think I have a few stuck to my ass." Laughing, I started grabbing some and taking them back to the file cabinet.

"Did you find out what happened to Kema?"

"Not yet, but I will." I tried my best to push away my thoughts. This was not another empty promise, he was going to find them.

"We have to find her parents. If we can't, we have to plan her funeral."

"Say less." Climbing in the bed beside him, I laid on his chest and tried to go to sleep, but flashes of Kema lying on the porch dying clouded my mind.

Mantico St. Lauren

Finally, shit been going good between me and Dany. These past few days been rough on her, but I did everything in my power to make sure Lil Mama was good. Since it happened, Dany been crying in her sleep hard as fuck. Only thing I could do was hold her. Shit, what can a nigga say to some shit like that? That was a hurt that would have to heal on its own. I know if something happened to Mink or Fil, a nigga would be fucked up. Only time and strength will heal her.

I was just glad she was allowing me to be there for her. I never would have thought the letters I wrote would have been the thing that brought us together. I never intended for her to see them, but when I walked in my room and saw them sprawled all over the bed I was good with it. Everything I said in them bitches, I meant. When she was away, it was the only thing that kept me focused. I knew I had to do it for her, and I did. Yeah, Manny was my pops and he handed it over to me, but I had to work hard to keep that shit going. When you're on top, everybody wants what you have. You have to make sure your team loyal and not trying to cross you or takeover. I was built for the shit, but the stress of it all can become overwhelming. Writing Dany became my peace. It was the only way I could unwind or actually get out what I was feeling.

"Can we go out to dinner tonight? I'm tired of sitting in the house crying and planning this funeral. I need some air." This was the first time she spoke of going outside, so I was down with that shit. I left every day hitting the streets with Mink trying to figure out what happened to Kema, but we came up empty every time.

"We can go wherever you want to Lil Mama. Go get dressed." Climbing on top of me, she kissed me all over my face.

"Thank you Mantico." When she licked her lips after saying my name, my dick bricked up.

"Keep that shit up only thing you gone be eating is this dick, Lil Mama. I know you feel this bitch lifting you in the air. Go play with something safe before you be playing with these baws in your jaws." She laughed, but I was dead serious. Getting up, she ran out the room and I went in the closet to grab some clothes. I'm sure it was hot as fuck outside, hell it was always hot in Chicago during July, so I grabbed some shorts and a T shirt. Throwing them on, I looked for some gym shoes to slide on when my doorbell rang. I had no idea who it was, but I was assuming it was Mink. He was the only one that was crazy enough to pop up at my shit unannounced.

Running downstairs, I opened the door and instantly became stressed when I saw it was Celeste. I had been so caught up in Dany, I forgot all about her ass. I know I told her to take some time, but I hadn't officially broken things off. The shit happened with Kema, and I just threw myself into Dany. Celeste hadn't even crossed my mind. She pushed past me and walked inside.

"Tico, why haven't I heard from you?" She didn't know it, but that question was a lot harder to answer than she thinks.

"It's a lot of shit going on right now, Celeste. I'll call your phone and we can sit down and talk, but right now, is not a good time." Rolling her eyes, she ignored what I was saying.

"It's never a good time for you Tico. Look, I know a lot has been said and done, but we have gone through too much to end like this. Tico, you know how I feel about you. I'm sorry for all the stress I've been causing." Walking over to me, she grabbed me and pulled me into a hug. I know she wasn't wrong in all this, I just needed time to figure some shit out.

"I know. Just give me a few days. Everything will be back to normal by then and I'll have time to talk." She was still holding me when she leaned down and kissed me.

"Well, ain't this some cozy shit." Closing my eyes, I cursed the fucking Gods. Them mufuckas had to hate my ass or something.

"Dany, go back upstairs. I'll be up in a minute." She scoffed and stormed to the kitchen.

"This lil fat bitch just thinks this is her house now huh? I thought you said you only needed a few days before you put the trash out." Drawing my hand back, I was about to knock this bitch to the moon and back, when Dany practically snatched me back. I was sick of her disrespecting Lil Mama, so I was about to knock her lips closed.

"Aht aht. You ain't never gotta hit a bitch when I'm in the room." Before I could say anything else, Dany hit Celeste so hard, I was stunned. She never stopped hitting her, and all Celeste could do was drop to the ground and ball up. I assumed Dany couldn't fight because she let so much shit slide. But she was on demon time right now and I couldn't let it continue.

"Aight, that's enough." When she turned around to look at me, Lil Mama made me step back. It's like she checked out.

"Oh, you defending this bitch. You want me to stop fucking yo lil girlfriend up. Fuck you and this duck face hoe. How bout that." She kicked her again and walked out the door. I knew she needed me to drop her off, so I helped Celeste of the floor.

"I told yo ass it wasn't a good time. Now look at you. In here with yo lip on yo wig and shit. Get yo ass up. I'll call you in a few days." I could tell she wanted to talk shit, but it probably hurt since her lip was so swollen. Hearing a crash, I let her go and ran outside. My garage door was in the driveway and Dany was swerving down the street in my fucking car, almost on top of my neighbor's grass. Knowing she couldn't drive I ran in the house to get another set of keys. Hell, she could have taken the truck I bought her, but she wanted to fuck my shit up.

"Get the fuck up Celeste, damn. All that shit you talked, you would at least think yo knees wouldn't give out when a bitch hit yo ass." I grabbed the keys to my truck and ran back towards the front. Celeste was slowly standing, but I needed to catch Dany before she killed herself. Grabbing her by the collar, I dragged her ass out my house and locked the door.

"Really Tico." Not bothering to answer her, I ran over to the garage and jumped in the truck. I took off like a bat out of hell in the direction I saw Dany going. About five blocks down, I saw my Lambo crashed into a pole and my heart fell in my ass. Fuck! God please let her be okay. Throwing my truck in park, I jumped out and ran towards the car. She was sitting there looking dumb as fuck and I couldn't do shit but shake my head.

"You aight?"

"Yeah." It took everything in me not to laugh.

"Then bring yo dumb ass on. Gone storm the fuck out like you know how to drive. You paying for that mufucka in pussy, just so you know." Walking off, I got back in my truck and waited for her to come. This mufucka got out and had the nerve to be stomping. One of her shoes was gone, and she had a slight limp. Her hair was fucked up and her lip was bleeding.

You would think her ass just got beat up from the way she was looking. Paired with that dumb ass look on her face, I finally fell out laughing. When she got in the truck, she slammed the door and looked at me.

"You think this shit funny, but we gone see who gets the last fucking laugh. Go find my fucking shoe, ugly ass hoe." Laughing hard, I got out of the truck trying to find this ugly ass shoe. It was lodged under the car, so I grabbed it and walked back over.

Danyelle Blakely

"You sure you want to go to this party? We don't have to go Dany." I had been doing alright, but today was bad for me. Every time I tried to open my mouth, I cried. I really didn't want to go out, but I did some shit to get back at Tico, and I needed to see the fallout from it.

"Yeah, I'm about to go get ready. I need to get out of this house, and you need to get out and do something other than killing people." Even though he was searching high and low, it was still no news on who killed Kema.

"I hope you like the dress moms sent over, but if you come down looking like Blanch, you going by yo damn self." Tico smiled at me as his grey eyes pierced through me. I could tell he wanted to get some shit started, but I was ready to go be petty. That day I crashed his car, he found the shit real funny. I told him I was going to get his ass back, and that's just what the fuck I did.

"Fuck you, Tico. I'll be ready in like an hour." Leaving out his room, I headed towards my room and jumped in the shower. I was careful not to wet my hair, because I needed this shit to act right. When I was done handling my hygiene, I got out and did a slight beat on my face. I wasn't into all that other shit, but it was a black-tie party, so I needed to look the part. Walking out the room, I looked at the red fitted silk dress and slid it on. It was thin strapped, so I decided to go with no bra. I could appreciate how she got me one that stopped at my knees since it was so hot outside. After I added a few curls in my hair, I threw on my strappy gold heels and I was done. I grabbed my gold clutch and walked out my room. I ran right into Tico.

"Damn." His grey eyes were all over me and I felt like I was popping my shit.

"You don't look so bad yourself Mr. St Lauren. Let me see you." His ass started walking like he was modeling, and I couldn't do shit but laugh. "You better walk that walk nigga." He started laughing as he held my waist leading me down the stairs. I felt like a princess in a fairytale, but this prince wasn't mine. I wasn't dumb. The only reason he's all under me was because of what happened to Kema. If it wasn't for that, he would be chasing behind that skinny ass bitch, Celeste. Not wanting to ruin my mood, I shook it off. Besides, I was going to get his ass back good tonight. Climbing in the car, I grabbed my phone and checked my messages. I wanted to make sure everything was a go, and when I saw that it was, I smiled to myself.

"You good over there? It better not be a nigga making you smile. I'll drown you in my mama's pussy. Try me." I turned to look at him like he was crazy.

"Nigga, I don't want to be nowhere near yo mama's old ass pussy."

"I'm telling her what you said. Just wait til we get there. You know Yvette from the hood. I don't think you can lay her out like you did Celeste. She got them hands."

"Don't get Vette dropped around this bitch. My hands don't have a perspective person. They will drop anybody around this bitch. Even you."

"Naw. As soon as you come at me, I'mma slap you in yo head with this big ass dick. Now shut the fuck up." I just nodded allowing him to think he won. We pulled up to the house and it was way more alive than the last time. It was cars all around the winding driveway, valet workers, and the house looked alive. This was my first party, and I was excited as hell. Tico put his arm around my waist and walked me inside. It was so many people, and everyone was looking good dressed up. Yvette and Manny walked over to us, and we all embraced.

"I didn't know if you would come. I'm so sorry to hear about your friend. Let me know if you need any help with the arrangements." Giving a fake smile, I grabbed one of the champagne glasses from a waiter quick. Who the fuck brings that shit up at a party? I know she meant well, but I was trying not to think about that right now.

"Yeah, I needed to get out the house. Just wanted to take my mind off it for a while."

"Exactly Yvette. Bring yo ass on talking about death at damn party. Ass ain't got no manners," Manny yelled at her as he pulled her away. She turned back to me mouthing sorry and I smiled at her.

"Let me find out you really trying to beef with my moms. I don't mind jumping you with her." I was about to talk shit when I heard my phone going off. Sending a quick message, I grabbed another drink. "Naw for real. Who the fuck keeps texting yo phone? I told you that shit was only for emergencies and I'm standing right here." Shrugging my shoulders, I took a sip and looked around the room.

"Well, you should have bought me a real one then. Like I said, I'm not yo bitch. Hell, she might be here. You might want to go look around instead of standing over here hovering and shit." I could see his jaw jumping as he walked off. He didn't go far though, just enough to give me some space. When my text came through and said he was here, I told him where to come and I pulled my phone out ready to record this shit. Some fine ass nigga walked over to Tico, and I hit record as I moved closer.

"Hey babes. It's nice to finally meet you." His arm draped towards Tico's waist and this nigga was looking stunned as fuck.

"Nigga, what the fuck you just say to me?"

"I said, it's nice to finally meet you. These past couple of days were rough on me." Tico looked around trying to make sure nobody heard this shit, and I couldn't stop laughing.

"Tico, who is your friend?" Manny walked up looking at him with the side eye.

"I'm Daniel, Tico's date." Yvette choked on her drink, and I had tears rolling down my face I was laughing so hard.

"Nigga, are you high? I've never met you a day in my life and if yo lil fairy ass wanna skip until tomorrow, you better get the fuck out my face." Tico was pissed but trying not to cause a scene.

"Of course we never met in person. We've talked online for the past couple of days though. You're the one that invited me here. Saying how you couldn't wait to introduce me to everyone, and how you was going to blow my back out after. If you're still in the closet, I can't do this shit. I'm not fucking with another nigga scared to tell his parents he sucks ass." Tico grabbed his gun and put it to Daniel's head.

"Nigga, do I look like a fucking booty bandit to you? I've never talked to you, and I didn't invite you." Daniel reached in his pocket and grabbed his phone.

"Cus see what we not finna do is make Daniel look like a liar. Mmmk. Is this not you boo boo? Is this not you? Are these not messages back and forth between us?" Tico snatched the phone and scrolled through.

"Tendermeat.com. Son, what the fuck is this? I mean if you gay, just say that shit. Don't be causing no scene at our party. Take yo lover and go outside. Handle this shit. NOW!" Manny was pissed.

"If you don't want Peter Pan dead in the middle of your dance floor, you better get him the fuck out of here. You know damn well I ain't signed up on no fucking site."

"Daniel, why don't you follow me son," Yvette said still shocked.

"I can't believe I done wasted my time and my damn gas. Fake gay ass thug. He fine though mama, but I'm pissed."

"I know. I know." Yvette was talking to Daniel as she directed him out the door. Tico turned to me and saw me recording with tears in my eyes. He looked at me confused at first and then fell out laughing.

"Oh, you think this shit funny? Why would you do that Dany, you almost got that nigga killed in this bitch."

"Naw, don't come over here now gay boy. Your lover outside waiting on you. He said don't play with him." Manny was looking confused, but I was laughing too hard to explain.

"Anybody want to explain to me what's going on?"

"This simple mufucka got mad at me for laughing at her, so she put my info on a gay dating site and had the nigga meet us here." Manny face went from shock to bright red, and then he fell out laughing. "I'm glad yall think it's funny, but I'mma take that shit out on that pussy tonight. You like ass so much, it's time for you to see what that be like." Manny turned his face up and walked off. I was turned on and nervous at the same time.

Mantico St. Lauren

Tapping on Dany's door, I tried to see if she was ready. The services for Kema were starting soon, and she still hadn't come out of the room. We had no luck finding her parents, so it was on us to handle the arrangements. I tapped again and leaned closer to the door to see if I could hear her. When I heard nothing, I slowly turned the knob. I stuck my head in the door, but I didn't see her.

"Hey, Lil Mama. We gotta get out of here if we want to make it in time." She didn't respond, so I stepped completely in the room. Looking around, I was shocked to find her balled up in the corner on the floor crying. "Fuck." Walking over, I sat down beside her and pulled her to my chest. Wrapping my arms around her, I held her as she cried.

"Why did they have to take her? She didn't bother anybody. Now I'm alone and I don't have anybody." Hearing her feel like she was around this bitch by herself had me feeling a way. I've been trying to show her I'm here for her, but she still didn't trust me. I had no idea what it was going to take, but she was not trying to let a nigga in. Clearing my throat, I tried to make sure she couldn't hear the disappointment in my voice.

"You got me Dany. I'm here."

"I can't see her go in the ground. I can't bury my heart. I just can't do it." Grabbing her by the chin with one hand, I used my other to wipe her tears away.

"You can. It's going to be hard, but you got this. You're one of the strongest people I know. You have already been through a lot, but you're still standing. It's one of the reasons why you're different." She tried to drop her head, but I pushed it back up. "Hey, and even if you get weak and start to fall, I'll be there to hold you up." Standing up, I grabbed her hand and pulled her off the floor. "I'll be your footprints in the sand." She looked at me funny but walked out with me. Heading downstairs, I grabbed my keys, and headed into the garage. My door was still gone, and I was lucky to be in this boujie ass neighborhood. The workers were coming out tomorrow to fix it, so I wasn't pressed.

Opening her door, I waited for her to get in before I went to my side and climbed in. Not having to worry about a door, I reversed out and headed towards the gravesite. Since it wouldn't be that many people, we decided to do the services like the white people. Everything would be done at the cemetery.

"What did you mean by footprints in the sand?" I turned to look at her and she was staring at me confused.

"My moms used to have this plaque hanging on her wall. It said some shit like they were asking the Lord why when they were at their weakest points or hardest times in their life, they would look and only see one set of footprints. They was asking him why he always leave them alone when they need him most. He responded saying it was only one set of footprints because during those times, I carried you." Tears were rolling down her face as she nodded.

"One set of footprints," she said as if she was taking it in. Reaching over, I grabbed her hand and held it.

"I will carry you Lil Mama. I got you." The rest of the ride was silent. I wish we could go back to the dinner party yesterday. I know she was still hurting and grieving, but for a moment she forgot about everything and allowed herself to laugh. Yeah, that shit she pulled was fucked up and I really should have dragged her by her nose hairs, but it made her laugh. I would give anything to see her smiling right now. I knew that shit wasn't about to happen though, since we were pulling up at the cemetery. Getting out, I walked around the car and opened her door. Taking a deep breath, she climbed out. She was walking slowly almost as if she didn't want to make it over to the site, but I kept pulling her.

"Who are all these people?" I smiled seeing the crew there showing their support.

"They work for me. They all knew and loved Kema. I didn't expect them to show up, but I'm glad they did." We took our seats, and the preacher began. I could feel Dany shaking, so I draped my arm around her and held her close. I knew it was nothing I could say that would make her pain go away, but I wanted her to know she was not alone. Glancing over at Mink, I felt bad for my nigga. I think he liked her a lot more than he let on. His ass was over there tore up. Shit, this was the first time I've ever seen him cry. I hated feeling useless, and that's why I needed to find whoever did this shit. At least I will be able to say I gave my nigga and Dany some type of peace.

"What the fuck?" Dany said and pulled away from me. I looked around trying to figure out what upset her, and I instantly got pissed.

"Not today Satan." Standing up, I walked over towards Celeste. "What are you doing here?" Mufucka was dressed like she was going to a prom rather than a funeral.

"So, I can't be here for my man, and he lost someone?" I could feel the heat from behind me, so I knew Dany was approaching us.

"Either you drag this bitch up out of here or I will. If I drag her, she going in one of these holes." I could understand why Dany was pissed, but I also understood why Celeste thought it was okay for her to be here.

"Celeste, out of respect for Dany I have to ask you to leave. This is her sister, and I don't have any control over who can and can't be here." It was the nicest way I could put this shit, but I could tell she was still pissed about it.

"Wow. When you're done with this, come see me."

"I'll be there." Dany turned and looked at me like I had two heads. Ignoring that, I tried to grab her hand, but she snatched away. We took our seats, and I nodded to the preacher to continue. He wrapped it up and grabbed a box of doves. Dany stood and took the box from him.

"Best, you always said you were a free spirit. Never wanting anything to hold you back or hold you down. You just wanted to li-..." Dany's words got caught in her throat as she choked back tears. "You just wanted to live. Baby girl, I don't know how I'mma get through life without you, but I'm going to live for you. I will keep your memories alive, and I promise you that Tico is going to send you some company." The preacher looked shocked, but I was happy as fuck that she knew I was going to keep my word. Opening the box, she allowed the doves to fly free.

The workers started lowering the casket, so we all stood and threw our roses in one by one. As each person dropped their rose, they left and went back to their cars. Mink walked off and I didn't get a chance to rap to him, but I would stop by his spot after I dropped Dany off. I knew Celeste was waiting on me, but my people needed me. Besides, the shit I had to say to her she wasn't gone wanna hear it. After a while, me and Dany were the only two left at the site and I didn't know how to tell her it was time to go.

She was crying so hard, she almost made me cry with her ass. Her body began to shake, and I could see that she was about to drop to the ground. Grabbing her, I picked her up, and carried her towards the car. I could feel her tears on my neck rolling down hot and fast. Opening the door, I placed

her inside, walked around and climbed in.

"Footprints in the sand." I looked at her and grabbed

her hand.

"Always Lil Mama."

"Why you going to your room?" Tico asked me that as if I he thought I was going to do something to myself if I was alone. I just kind of wanted my space to be in my thoughts.

"Just wanted some time, Tico. If you want me under you, just say dat. You ain't gotta be treating me like I'm suicidal or something." He walked over to me and leaned down to give me a kiss.

"If I thought you was suicidal, I would be trying to get some pussy one last time. I just don't want you alone in your thoughts. That shit not healthy. I know it hurts, but if you're alone and crying all day, you will never start to heal." I understood what he was trying to do, so I gave in.

"Okay, but you not getting no pussy. I don't trust you after that Daniel shit. You might try to go in my ass." He laughed as we walked towards his room.

"That's my shit. I can get that pussy anytime I want it. Remember that. Besides, you be the one constantly trying to fuck. A nigga be tired." We walked in his room, and he took off his shirt. I couldn't take my eyes off him, but I refused to make a move. Grabbing one of his t shirts, he threw it at me.

"You know you not getting in my shit with all them clothes on. Plus, I need to rub on them thick ass thighs." Giggling, I removed my clothes and put his shirt on. They always fit me tight and stopped right at the bottom of my ass. Climbing in his bed, I got under the covers. His ass loved the air on high, but I was cold.

"Since we didn't have a repast, can you order something to eat? I'm kind of hungry and you better find something good on tv since you want me in here under yo ass." Shaking his head, he grabbed his phone. "Oooh, can we get seafood?"

"Yo ain't eating that fishy shit in my bed. We can do that tomorrow. When you go to a repast, you supposed to eat soul food. So, we're going to get drinks and shit and have Kema repast right here. You can tell me stories of yall acting an ass and shit." I wanted to cry, but I fought them back. He didn't know, but this was the best gift he could have ever given me. That's all I kept telling myself is I needed more time. This helps with that.

"Okay. Her favorite drink was Malibu mixed with Ciroc, so that's what we drinking tonight." I could tell he didn't want that, but oh well. It was what we were having. He was on his phone about ten minutes making all this happen and I waited anxiously for him to come over. Finally, he threw on some basketball shorts and made his way to the bed.

"Aight, while we waiting on the food and shit to come, tell me a story. Not no boring shit either. Give me something funny."

"So, one day while you were out running behind yo lil bitch. Kema came over and attempted to teach me how to drive. Thinking about that day had me in tears from laughter.

"Aight Best. This nigga keep leaving the house and shit, you gotta know how to drive so you can follow his ass. He bought you this truck, so we gone put it to good use."

"How is following a nigga that ain't mine good use?"

"Easy bitch. If you keep beating him and that hoe ass, he will eventually stop going. Fuck all that. We will work on how to hook him later. First, we gotta teach you how to drive so you can follow him. All around the mulberry dick, Dany chased Ticoooo. Dany thought it was all in fun, then pop goes the pussssy." I looked at her like she was crazy.

"Bitch, did you really change that nursery rhyme to some shit like that? You're sick in the head."

"And you're stalling. Put the shit in drive and go around this parking lot. Act as if you're on the street, so use your turn signals and all." I nodded and moved the gear shift. The car shot backwards, and she started screaming. "Brake bitch. BITCH BRAKE."

"I am." I wasn't though, the damn car kept going backwards. Slamming into another car was the only thing that stopped us.

"Aww hell naw. You trying to kill me. Get the fuck out my shit right now."

"Best, give me one more chance." I was laughing hard, but her ass was shaking.

"If you don't get yo ass out, you walking home. Lesson is over. Let that nigga teach you. For now, you can catch the bus or an Uber to follow his ass." I couldn't stop laughing and I couldn't stop the tears falling from my eyes. She was so serious. Kema jumped out the car looking shook the fuck up. Climbing out, I walked over to the other side and got in. When she put the car in drive, I looked at her crazy.

"You not gone wait for them or leave your insurance information?"

"Bitch, you a felon on papers and no license. Yo ass going to jail if they catch us. Now put yo seatbelt on so I can get us out this jam. Dumb ass see that big ass R and think you going forward. Whew chile, I can not."

"Tico, I was laughing so hard, I almost pissed on myself." He was laughing too, and he was right. Talking about her and acting like we were at a repast was better for me.

"One thing Kema was gone do was beg. When you got locked up, that girl made me feed her like she was really my friend. Kept saying, but I'm your Best. Don't do me like that." Knowing how she was, I already knew she gave him a hard time.

It seemed like we were talking for hours when the doorbell rang. Tico went downstairs to get our stuff and I laid back with the biggest smile on my face. He told me stories about how Kema came from visiting me and would try to fight him and then beg for some money. It felt good to know how much my Best loved me. He walked back in the room with the food, and I couldn't wait to dig in. We continued to talk while we ate and had some drinks. As soon as we started to wind down, he got up and started to get dressed.

"Where the fuck you going, Tico?"

"I gotta run to make. I won't be gone long. I promise we can continue when I get back. Just give me a few hours." Leaning down, he kissed me, but he had me fucked up.

"Yeah, okay." Shaking his head laughing, he headed out the door. Remembering that Celeste asked him to come over, I got pissed. He thought he was gone keep laying up with me and then running to that bitch, he had me fucked up. I needed a reason to make him leave her and show him I'm not that bitch at the same time. I sat and thought for a while as I continued to drink. The more I drank, the crazier my thoughts became. Getting up, I looked in his drawers and found a bunch of credit cards. I saw them when I was looking for some mail. Grabbing one, I downloaded Uber to my phone and typed in his information. Throwing on some clothes, I pulled my hair back in a ponytail, grabbed the bottle of Ciroc, and went downstairs to wait on my ride.

The more I thought about how he had me fucked up, the more I drank. His ass was trying me, but I was about to show him. My ride pulled up, so I got inside. It didn't take long to pull up to his parent's house.

"Don't pull off." My words slurred as I yelled at the Uber driver. Getting out, I walked to the door and started banging on it. Yeah, I liked Yvette, but she was the bitch that had this disrespectful nigga. The door opened and I put the bottle up to her head. "You going with me. This a kidnap bitch." She looked at me confused, but I wasn't playing with her ass. I was drunk as fuck, but I could still take her old ass.

"Danyelle, are you drunk?"

"Yeah, but what'sssss drunk got to do with it. Got to do with it." I started singing it like Tina Turner and she started laughing. "Don't laugh, bitch. It's a kidnap. Let's go. If your son want you back, he gone have to leave that skinny ass bitch and come get you." I wasn't sure since I was so tipsy, but I think I saw amusement on her face.

"You kidnapping me in an Uber?"

"Yeah boy. You ready?" We got inside and I told the driver to take us to a motel. He did as I asked and I continued to sip my bottle. "Yo son got me fucked up. I bet he come now with his ugly big dick ass. Why yo son thing so big?" She chuckled, but I didn't find shit funny.

Mantico St. Lauren

"Bro, what is the purpose of life?" Mink was looking to me for answers I couldn't give. He was looking for some type of peace and nothing I said was going to help him.

"Man, who the fuck knows. I just try to live my life to the fullest, learn from my lessons, get money and one day I'm gone die."

"We kill people for sport, but good people seem to die. They can live their entire life doing the right thing, and car slide off the road then they gone. Look at Kema. She never hurt nobody, and she get killed. What kind of shit is that?" I thought about what he said long and hard before I responded.

"Sometimes, it's just a freak accident. You will never get any answers from it. But sometimes. Sometimes that shit is your karma. Kema didn't do shit, but you did. Maybe it was God's way of getting back at you. The people we kill be fucked up individuals. When they ain't shit, most of the time they families don't know it. We inflict hurt on them, so one day that shit gotta come back. Hell, think about how many people we done killed trying to find out what happened to Kema. It was probably some innocent mufuckas in that batch. We shouldn't decide who gets to live and die, but we do. You think somebody else out there not playing God?" He looked at me and nodded before taking another drink.

"Makes sense. I just wish this didn't have to be my karma. They could have taken my baby mama or something. Bitch is stressful." We both laughed at that. "What if your girl is your karma?"

"I'll find a way to live with it. I'm gone tear this bitch up, but I can't stop living. She wouldn't want that for me. I know what you going through is hard, especially because yall didn't really get any time, but it will get better. You just have to want it to get better."

"I'm not gone be good until I find out what happened to her. That's the only way I'll get peace. Either I'mma keep killing until I find out what happened, or a mufucka gone kill me. At least if they kill me, I'll be able to ask her." We laughed again, but it was one of those that's fucked up but true laughs.

"We gone find out nigga. That's my word. Dany going through it too." Mink looked at me confused.

"I was fucked up at the funeral, but I meant to ask you. Are you and Celeste still together or is it you and Dany now?"

"I gotta have a talk with Celeste, but I'm with Dany. Lil Mama is too good for me to keep stringing her along. I fucked up with her once, I'm not gone make the same mistake twice. You feel me?"

"Yeah, I feel that shit. What we gone do about the connect though?"

"Whatever we have to do. If he pulls out because I don't want to be with Celeste, then we will find another connect. Nobody owns me, and I refuse to let anyone force me into some shit." As soon as I said that a text came through from Dany.

LIL MAMA: IF YOU WANT TO SEE THE BITCH YO MAMA AGAIN, YOU BETTA COME MEET ME BITCH. I read the text like ten times to see if I was reading it right. Someone must have Dany as well because it doesn't make sense why she would be texting me that.

ME: WHERE YOU WANNA MEET?

LIL MAMA: BITCH I DO THE ASKING WHEN IT'S TIME TO ASK. MEET ME AT MOTEL 6 ON LINCOLN. TIME IS TICKING.

"Grab yo burner and let's go." I jumped up fast and practically ran out the door.

"Nigga, slow down. What the fuck is going on? Yo ass looking like a strong ass build a bear right now."

"Somebody kidnapped Dany and my moms." As soon as he heard that, he stopped laughing. I took off like a bat out of hell.

"Karma." Was all Mink said. It was only an hour drive, but it seemed like it took two. So much was going through my mind and all I could do was hope they were okay. I pulled up and jumped out barely parking. Grabbing my burner out my waist, I walked towards the door of the room that was given.

Mink was beside me ready as well. Pointing my gun at the door, I knocked. When it opened Dany was looking at me shocked. I looked around to check out the surroundings before stepping inside. My moms was eating some chicken and it looked like they were playing cards.

"Where are they?"

"Who?" They both asked at the same time.

"The nigga that kidnapped yall?" Mink went to check the bathroom, but from the look on his face, I could tell nobody was here.

"You looking at her. Dany kidnapped me from the house at bottle point in an Uber." I was confused, but I had to hear this.

"Wait, what?"

"You heard what she said bitch. You thought you was gone run to that hoe, so I made you come to me." I looked at Mink and he fell the fuck out laughing.

"Ma, explain to me what happened. You're sober and maybe you can make sense of this. You let her kidnap you with a bottle and in an Uber?"

"Yup. I mean, she wanted her man. I don't like Celeste, and I don't appreciate you playing with Dany's feelings. You want a wing? These thangs is fye."

"Who paid for the room?" I asked, but I think I already know the answer to that.

"I did son."

"So, yo slow ass paid for your own kidnapping." Moms threw a bone at me and hit me in the head with it.

"Watch yo mouth."

"Man, bring yall dumb asses on. I can't believe yall got me out here about to kill everybody on the road for this bullshit. I wasn't even with Celeste. I was with Mink. Yall forgot, he lost Kema too." Dany mouth made an O shape, but all I could do was shake my head. I wasn't gone let them live this down for a while. It was funny now, but my nerves were still shot so I was slow to laughing at this shit.

"Ma, don't forget the wings and the bottle. I'm hungry." Dany was slurring as she stumbled towards me. Putting my arm around her waist, I led her outside. I'm just glad she was okay. We all climbed in my car, and I headed towards my parent's house to drop my moms off. "Babbbyy. You gone fuck me good tonight?" I almost choked on my spit. I looked in the rearview and my moms was chuckling. She found this shit funny.

"Hey bro, you got one on your hands." This time, I laughed as well because he wasn't lying.

"I'm already knowing. I got a trick for her ass though."

"Meoowww. What's newwww pussy cat? This nigga finna whoooaa whoaaaa whoaaaaa." The entire car laughed at Dany and five minutes later she was snoring. I pulled up at my parent's house and got out to walk her to the door.

"Son, I hope you do right by this one. She is the one for you. I know it."

"Even though she kidnapped you?"

"That was a strong come with me, not a kidnapping. Besides, yo father texted me as soon as I got in the car. I told him what was going on." I looked at her crazy.

"So, you couldn't tell me? Yall scared the shit out of a nigga."

"She wanted her man, so I stayed put. Just remember what I said. She's the one."

"I know. I'm cutting things off with Celeste tomorrow. Thank you for everything."

"Thank me with a new Birkin bag. See you soon." She walked in the house, and I shook my head. Walking back to the car, I wondered how this shit was going to play out. I had a feeling Celeste was gone make me body her ass. Opening the door, I stepped inside, and Lil Mama was snoring like it was ten grown men in this mufucka.

"Bro, call me an Uber. I'm not driving an hour listening to this shit. Shorty rocking the car and shit." We both laughed and I drove towards my house.

"You can take the car. I'll get it from you tomorrow. I'm putting her ass in the basement tonight." When I pulled up to my house, I got out and grabbed Lil Mama. She didn't even stir as I picked her up to carry her inside.

"God damn yo back strong as fuck and where the hell yo garage door?"

"Karma." When I said that, he fell out laughing and I headed in the house. I thought I was getting some pussy, but a nigga ain't even want this drunk shit.

Danyelle Blakely

Looking around, I was laid on the floor with a blanket thrown over me. My back and my head was pounding and I realized I was on Tico's floor in the foyer. Right at the fucking front door. The last thing I remember was falling asleep in his car, so I have no idea how I got right here. Getting up, I damn near crawled to the kitchen to get some water. A bitch was happy as hell I smelled food. Tico was sitting at the table eating and my stomach growled loud as hell.

"If you down here eating, that mean you had to step over my ass to get in here. Did you really just leave me on the fucking floor? Plus, how the hell did I end up on the floor in the first place?" He took a sip of his juice before he answered me.

"I dropped you right there. You wanted to be tough Judy last night, so I figured you could get yourself to the room. When I came down this morning and saw you shaking on the floor, I got you a blanket." Rolling my eyes, I went in the fridge and grabbed a water. Walking over to the stove, I looked in the pots, but it was no food. Opening the microwave and stove, I noticed they both was empty.

"So, you didn't make me nothing to eat?" I damn near had tears in my eyes when I realized that shit.

"I mean, you can make you something. It's shit in there to cook." I looked at him in disbelief. He knows how I feel about food and his petty ass did this to me.

"Wow. I guess all that shit you was talking was bullshit. I mess up one time and this how you do me." He looked at me shocked.

"Mufucka you tried to kidnap my moms. What kind of shit is that? If you wanted to know where I was going, all you had to do was ask. What if something would have happened to yall?" Shifting from foot to foot, I dropped my head embarrassed.

"Ion know. I was drunk Mantico. You the one kept pushing them shots down my throat. Can I have a piece of your bacon and one pancake?" He tried to hold it in but fell out laughing.

"Girl, yo food in the dining room on the table. Soft ass about to cry over some food." I ain't care what he said about me at that point. I knew I had food. Taking off running, I grabbed my plate and came back to the table with him. Sitting down, I grabbed his cup and drank some of his juice.

"What are we going to do about the condo? You bought it for me, and I haven't stayed in it one night." He shrugged his shoulders and kept eating.

"If you saying you wanna stay here with me, that's cool. We can put it back on the market. I'm not pressed for money. If you wanna go live there, I'll come over every night and get some pussy. It's up to you." I wasn't sure what I wanted to do. Was it too soon to move in with him?

"Are you still going to date Celeste?" He looked at me with a weird look on his face.

"She on her way over here. Actually, she should be pulling up any minute." Fire went through my body, and I wanted to beat his ass. Grabbing his cup of juice, I threw it in his face. Jumping up, he ran up on me and grabbed me around my neck hard as fuck.

"I swear I don't want to hurt you, but you keep fucking trying me. If you want to know something, ask me. Quit assuming shit or you gone lose me. All this toxic shit you be on, that ain't my style. Use your words or I'mma use these hands. You get me?" I fought back the tears and tried to calm my anger. I wanted to punch his ass in the face, but I went with another tactic.

"Why the fuck would you bring her here? Are you trying to hurt me?" He released me and walked back to his seat.

"I asked her here because I didn't want to upset you by going to her house. I'm breaking it off with her." I felt like shit, but I wasn't about to apologize. Nigga just choked me, hell we even. Picking up my fork, I started eating my food.

"This shit good. Thank you." His ass laughed loud and hard.

"Your big back ass ain't gone apologize?"

"Nope. You could have said it all in one sentence what was happening. It ain't my fault you don't know how to serve tea right. Can you pass me some syrup?"

"I wish the fuck I would. I hope ain't no more in the bottle and you choke on that dry ass pancake." Laughing, I got up and grabbed it myself. Drowning my pancakes in it, I started back eating. Hearing the doorbell and knowing it was that bitch, I sat there and kept eating. That had nothing to do with me and Tico was gone have to handle that himself. At least that was what I thought until he walked in the kitchen with her.

"You have got to be kidding me. Look, the only reason I agreed to come over was to give you one last chance. I was going to call Julio and tell him we good and business could continue. However, I see that's not the case. You can keep your lil hood rat, but you just lost your connect."

"He don't care bitch. He was calling you over here to dump you. Now get yo stiff ass out of here before I drag you out." She looked at Tico to see if he was going to correct me.

"Fuck you looking at me for? You heard what my bitch said. Fuck out our shit." Celeste stormed off and I got up, made sure she was gone, came back to the kitchen and walked over to Tico.

"I liked that shit. Bend me over this table and fuck my insides loose." Doing as I asked, he pushed me over hard. Pulling my clothes down, he slid inside of me and took off.

"Damn, this pussy good as fuck."

"Mmm hmmm. Mmmm." He stopped pumping and I turned to look at him. "What?"

"I know you ain't just grab a piece of bacon while I'm hitting this pussy." Laughing, I slid a piece of pancake off the plate and stuffed it in my mouth.

"Okay, I'm done. Tear this pussy up." He stood there for a second I guess waiting to see what I was going to do. Right when I was about to say fuck it and grab another piece of bacon, he began stroking my pussy again. Not wanting to hurt his lil feelings, I pushed all thoughts of my food to the back of my mind and let him have his way.

"Lil Mama, you gotta throw this pussy back." I had no idea what that meant, so I pushed back towards him. I thought he was all the way in, but I guess not.

"You in now?"

"Mufucka I been in, that's not what that mean."

"Well, you ain't teach me this part. What am I supposed to do?"

"Rock back and forth and throw yo ass like you dancing." Slowly, I did what he said, and I finally caught a rhythm. "Yeah, like that. Can you do that shit and pick up the pace?" At first, it seemed hard, but the wetter my pussy got, the harder I wanted it, so I sped up some. I'm not sure if I was perfect at it, but I was doing good for my first time in my eyes.

"Mantico, oooh shit. Don't stop." My body was starting to shake, so I knew I was about to cum. Tico pulled out and I was about to go the fuck off when I felt his mouth on my pussy.

"If you cumming, then you gone do it in my mouth. I need to taste you." Hearing him say that had me shivering.

"Ooh baby. You can get all of fat ma. Eat that shit." I never knew this was what I was missing out on. If I had known sex was this good, I would have been gave this shit up. His tongue was moving so fast, all I could do was tuck my ass in and run. My body shook hard, and I could no longer hold it back.

"This shit taste so good." When his mouth moved from my pussy, I was about to get up and get back to my meal. Instead, I felt his dick slid back inside of me and I was spent. I had no more energy and it seemed as if he wanted all the smoke today. I came so hard; I couldn't even throw it back. My knees were shaking bad and trying to give out. I would probably make Bambi's mother proud with how bad my knees were at the moment. As if he could feel me about to pass out, Tico grabbed me around the waist and picked up the pace.

His strokes were long and powerful. My mouth was dry, and my pussy was in tears.

"Ugghhhhh, fuck!" His body shook and he fell on top of me.

"I know you lying. Nigga in two seconds we about to be on the floor. My knees begging for a seat." Laughing, he stood up. My weak ass practically rolled over to my chair and grabbed a piece of bacon. "Don't say shit, I need some energy. I need to try and redeem myself."

"Naw, you gotta go pack. We heading to Puerto Rico."

"Mantico. You lying. I know you fucking lying. Oh my God, we going on a baecation?" When he laughed under his breath, I knew it was some bullshit in the game.

"Naw, we going to see Julio. I know Celeste pulling out as my connect, but I'm going to tell him to his face I'm about to kill that bitch. If he objects, war it is." I looked at him like he was crazy.

"So, we going on his turf. To tell him you about to kill his people, and then we gotta get out alive?"

"Pretty much."

"Well then, I'm about to finish my meal. You not about to have me die on an empty stomach. What if ain't no food where we go after death?" His ass laughed hard and turned to walk off.

"Man, hurry the fuck up." Picking up my bacon, I bit it slowly. I was not in a rush to die. He was my man, and I was going to stick beside him, but I was going to take my time doing it.

Mantico St. Lauren

Getting off the plane, I grabbed Dany by her waist and walked to the car that was waiting for us. Her body was slightly shaking, so I could tell she was nervous. This was why I picked her. Even in a battle she thought we would lose; she was right here by my side willing to ride for a nigga. I don't think it's a bitch out here holding a candle to Dany.

Climbing in the car, I tried to clear my mind. I was walking into this shit with no weapons, so if shit took a turn for the worse, we were assed out. One thing I knew for sure was, I was going to protect Lil Mama at all costs. I don't give a fuck if I had to eat every bullet in that bitch, I was going to make sure not one touched her. I went over a million plans in my head, but none of that shit seemed like I would come out on top.

"Bae, you know I'm a little thick. And, I haven't worked out since I been home. So, if we end up having to run just remember footprints in the sand." I looked at her and pulled her close to me.

"Always, Lil Mama." We went silent and stayed that way until we pulled up to the compound. We went through a series of driveways before we pulled up to the back of the house. We were escorted out and led inside. The guard took us to an office, and we were seated.

"This is some dope shit. Can we get some guards and shit? I mean, I feel safe when you at home, but what about when you gone? We ain't even got cameras at the house. How the fuck you the king of the city, but don't even have a security system at home?"

"Living way out there, I never needed it. Nobody knows where I live. I'm very selective and I've been lucky enough to not have no shit happen at my front door." When I said that, I immediately regretted the words leaving my mouth. Her face changed and I knew she was thinking about Kema. "She wasn't shot at the house. Either way, I'm going to find out who the fuck did that shit."

"I know. Maybe it would have been some kind of clues. I just find that weird that somebody shot at you the same time Kema showed up at your door. Seems connected, don't you think?" Hearing her say that made a lightbulb go off in my head. I did have cameras at the warehouse though. Celeste showed up and got shot at, then I showed up and the same happened to me. I didn't think about the cameras because all of that shit happened with Kema. My mind been occupied with Dany ever since. This was the reason Celeste was a good fit for me, she just wasn't the one for me. Before Lil Mama came into the picture, I had it made.

She stayed in her place because she knew the lifestyle. Celeste never argued with me or tried me. Whenever I went over to her house or allowed her at mine, it was all smiles and catering. Don't get me wrong, I knew Dany was the one for me, but she has me fucking up. I could have been figured this shit out if I wasn't chasing up behind her. Me and Lil Mama was gone have to have a talk if we were really going to make this work.

"Sorry I've kept you waiting. Tico, would you like anything to drink?" Standing, I shook his hand and sat back down.

"Naw, I'm good. We can just get to it."

"I was surprised to hear that you were coming here. Is there a problem with the shipment? I thought we were good with the new amounts." Now I was confused, and I could feel Dany shifting in her seat. She only did that when she was nervous.

"Naw, the shipment is good. Our problem is Celeste." It's like we were playing tit for tat because this nigga was now looking at me confused.

"Why is that?"

"I know that's your people and I'm sure I will have to find a new connect, but Celeste has to go. I don't kill women, but I can't allow a mufucka to make threats against me or what's mine." He nodded but didn't say a word.

"Let me get this right. You flew across the country, walked into my home as my guest because you want to kill my people?"

"Exactly." He leaned his head back and laughed hard as hell. Dany's leg was shaking fast, and I almost wanted to pinch her behind her kneecap. "Nigga, I don't give a fuck about a Celeste. She was one of the girls that came around our parties. Kind of became a regular. I introduced you two because I was trying to get you laid. You were so business all the time, trying to build an empire so you didn't let the lil chick in jail down. I was shocked to find out yall were an item, but hey who am I to say who should fall in love. Celeste hit me up and said you preferred her to be our middle man, and I was good with that as long as you weren't on no flaw shit." I ignored the fact that this fat ass mufucka called me a nigga and stood up.

"Aight Julio, thanks." He was still laughing, but I didn't find shit funny.

"You on your way to kill the bitch huh?"

"Do you like tortillas?" We both laughed and I grabbed Dany's hand and pulled her up.

"I know you're angry and I'm not asking you to spare her life. I just want you to chill out for a few days. You flew yo girl over here and it would be a shame not to show her how beautiful it is here. You all can be a guest in my home. What's mine is yours. Stay a couple of days." I was about to decline until I saw Dany beaming. She did everything but jump up and down.

"Aight bet, but we want the full experience."

"I wouldn't have it any other way. Lupe, come show our guests to their home." I was confused on him saying home, but I rolled with it. "Let me know if you need anything. Me and the wife are going dancing at eight if you want to come."

"We'll meet you back over here." Lupe guided us towards what Julio called our home, and I'm not gone lie, I was impressed. Even though I would never buy something this big for just me, it was nice as fuck. Shit was like walking through an amusement park it was so big. When we ended up

outside, I admired the gardens and finally understood what

he meant by our home. Through the gardens was another

house and it was nowhere as big as the compound, but the

shit definitely didn't look like a guest house. This mufucka

Dany took off running and I was about to fuck her ass up.

When I made it inside, Lupe left us alone.

"Don't be running acting excited like we live in a damn

shoe box. Fuck wrong with you?" Waving me off, she ran from

room to room leaving me standing there feeling like I wasn't

shit. Women will sure humble the fuck out yo ass. She ran

towards me with her eyes big as fuck looking shocked.

"Our house sits on the beach. I can literally walk out

our door and we're on a fucking beach. Whew, you may not

have a shoe box, but you ain't got no beach. If you're the king

of the city, shouldn't this be how you live. It's what I always

imagined when reading those urban fiction books." She was

rambling and I went from shaking my head to laughing. Like I said, a woman will humble yo ass quick. I followed behind her to see what she was talking about, and I swear I was in awe.

"We definitely fucking out here tonight."

"I can't wait. It's a standstill tub in our bathroom, so I'm about to go soak this ass. Go find our bags, I'm not trying to be walking around Puerto Rico with my shit hanging loose." Grabbing her to me, I gripped her ass and covered her mouth with mine. "What was that for?"

"Being you. I'm glad I brought you. You can have all this shit and more Lil Mama. You deserve the world."

"Right now, I just want you to get my bags and find me some food. I can't go dancing on an empty stomach." Giggling, she ran off and went to our room. Shaking my head, I went the same way we came in and back through the main house. I saw Lupe in the foyer and stopped her.

"Hey, can you find the driver we had; I need my bags."

"Yes sir. I'll have someone bring them to you right away Mr. St Lauren." Nodding at her I walked off. I really didn't have time to be chilling on vacation, but I did say I wanted to make it up to Dany for what happened. That shit will be waiting for me when I got home. Heading to one of the rooms, I jumped in the shower. When I got out, I wrapped a towel around me and went to find Dany. Lil Mama was standing on the beach in a long ass yellow dress. Her hair was blowing in the wind and that shit looked sexy as fuck. The smile on her face had me staring at her smiling like a goofy ass nigga. When she turned to me, my dick bricked up.

Her thick ass took off running towards me and I never wanted to lose sight of this. This was how a nigga was supposed to feel when he looked at his girl. I could admit, I was content with Celeste, but I never felt like this. Dany finally made it over to me and jumped in my arms. I could tell she wasn't wearing any underwear and I was ready to fuck something.

"Let's go take a walk on the beach. I haven't done that since I was a kid." She didn't even wait on my answer, she just grabbed my hand and pulled me towards the water.

"Dany, I know you all excited and shit, but look down. A nigga don't have on any clothes. You want me walking around this bitch assed out?"

"You have on a towel. Besides, no one else has access but us." I looked around and didn't see anyone, so fuck it.

"Dany, did you have any other family?" She turned to look my way but continued to smile and walk. When she didn't respond, I assumed she didn't want to talk about it. Looking around, I took in the scenery and this shit seemed different now that I wasn't here on business. All the grinding I did, I never stopped to enjoy what I worked so hard for. I think this was the first time a nigga ever felt sand on his toes.

"My uncle didn't want me. He took the insurance money and I never heard from him again. It was the only family that I knew of. Kema was my family." When she said the last part, I hated I asked. I wasn't trying to take her mind back to that shit, especially since she was having such a good time. I was about to apologize when she kicked water up at me. Hitting me on my arm, she took off running towards the water. "Tag, you're it." Chasing behind her, I grabbed her and carried her into the water. Wrapping her legs around me, she placed a million kisses on my face.

"You sexy as fuck Lil Mama. Where did you get this dress?"

"Lupe brought us clothes to wear tonight. You have something too."

"Ain't no grown ass man about to be dressing me. Fuck I look like? Let's go, so we not late for dancing and shit. Just so you know, a nigga doesn't dance. So, don't get your ass in here asking me." She rolled her eyes and kissed me again.

"Your grey eyes look amazing in this light. I could stare at you forever." Hearing that shit had me ready to stay in and lay up in my pussy. Not bothering to put her down, I carried her back to the house and into the bedroom. Dropping her on the bed, she looked at me and laughed. "Don't wrinkle my dress. I have to wear this. You can get some pussy, but you still taking me out on the town. You're also going to dance and have fun. You work all day every day, you need a day of just fun. Besides, you said you owe me."

"Aight, one dance. Now shut the fuck up and give me some of this pussy." Opening her legs, she smiled at me waiting on me to enter her. I could get used to this.

Everything was absolutely beautiful here. I almost didn't want to go home, but I knew that wherever Tico went, I would want to be there. I don't know what it was, but this nigga was giving me life. Anytime I felt down or thought about Kema, I could look at him and instantly I would feel better. My heart ached so much, I craved to see him just so I could smile again.

"Dany, I just want to say you are absolutely gorgeous. I could never wear a dress like that. My big ass would eat that dress up. You hear me?" Julio's wife Nadine was saying to me smiling. I was shocked she was black, but she was being modest. She was absolutely gorgeous. Most people would kill to have someone like her.

"You know dang on well you are absolutely beautiful. I love your home, thank you for inviting us in." Nadine winked at me, and Julio smiled at her with so much love, it had me yearning for that shit. "I thought we were going out on the town; I didn't know you all had a club on your compound."

"Yeah, most of our workers are here twenty four seven. We don't want them to feel as if their entire life is catering to us. We try to make sure they know we care about them. So, we have a club, a stable for them to go horseback riding, they have jet skis and boats to go parasailing. All kinds of shit. They families all live on the compound, and when they are off work they live it up. Maybe you can convince Tico to come over more often." Julio was nothing like I made him out to be. I just knew his ass was going to kill us, but now we were living it up in his home.

"That's boss shit."

"So is realizing when you found the love of your life and do right by them." He nodded towards me, and I instantly became nervous. I had no idea how he was going to respond. I've always been open about how I felt about him, but I had no idea he even liked me a little until I read his letters.

"Yeah, I'm slow to the shit, but I think I done figured it out. When you find solace in someone, that shit speaks volumes. Lil Mama holds me down, so I'mma make sure I do right by her. I just gotta make sure I got enough food to feed her ass." He said that shit literally as I was putting a piece of fruit in my mouth. Everyone at the table laughed. Tico looked at me and just stared into my eyes. I couldn't stop the smile that spread across my face as he took my hand. "Come on Lil Mama, let's get this dance out the way."

"You better not step on my feet either." He laughed and it was good to see. The Tico I remembered from back in the day was always serious. Since I've been home, he jokes, laughs, and smiles all the time. It was good to see this side of him. Tico pulled me out on the dance floor, never taking his eyes off me. The music slowed down and I thought he was going to change his mind, but he pulled me close to him.

"You're so fucking beautiful. I'm sorry I never noticed before. I see you now though." His breath was dancing on my lips, and I couldn't imagine this moment with anyone else.

We moved to the song, and he never tore his eyes away from me. The way he held me close and stared at me, had my pussy jumping from under my dress.

"Umm, can we get the fuck up out of here now. Julio and them cool, but I need some more dick. First, you're going to eat this pussy. Grab some of that fruit though, for us to eat after." He laughed and pulled me away.

"Aight Julio, I'm out of here. I'll see you tomorrow or some shit." They gave us knowing looks, but we didn't give a fuck. We practically ran back to our guest house. When he didn't walk towards the bedroom, I wondered where he was taking me. Tico guided me towards the beach, and it was absolutely gorgeous at night. He took me right by the water and laid me down. I was nervous as fuck, and I had no idea why.

Tico pulled my dress over my head and the night air against my nipples had my pussy jumping. He slid inside of me, and I couldn't help but gasp. He always felt so big in the beginning, and I always had to get used to the size. I wanted him to take off in my pussy, but I guess tonight was one of those days he wanted to make love.

"Fuck you so damn sexy." I've never been insecure about my thickness, but I loved how Tico always made me feel like I had the baddest shape in the world. His hand caressed my body as if he was trying to memorize every part. The sounds of the water matched my pussy with each stroke and the shit was music to my ears, but I wanted more. I needed that raw demon sex. My pussy was throbbing and I needing him to beat my shit up.

"Mantico, can you fuck me. I know you all in love and shit, but I need to feel that dick moving my insides around." He looked at me and fell out laughing.

"Aight, but don't start that crying shit asking me to slow down." Pushing my legs back, he pushed inside of me hard. Gasping, I waited for the next movement and his ass finally took off. My moans and screams filled the air, and I was loving every minute of it, until something went wrong. I had no idea what the fuck was happening, but the shit was burning, and it hurt bad.

"Tico, stop. Pull out for a second." He thought I was being a pussy, so this nigga smiled and started slamming his dick in me hard and fast. It felt like sandpaper was rubbing my shit and I had tears in my eyes.

"This dick good as fuck ain't it. Don't cry now, you gone take all this. I told yo ass." This nigga was feeling cocky but had no idea he was giving me a fucking driveway in my pussy.

"TICO STOP!" When I said it like that, he stopped moving and stared at me. "Nigga, you don't feel that sand in my pussy? This shit hurts and it burns." Out of nowhere, he started laughing hard as hell. Moving from on top of me, he stood up and kept laughing like the shit was funny. "Help me up, I gotta shake this shit from out of me." This nigga was laughing so hard, when he grabbed my hand, he slid me across the sand on my ass. Now the shit was in my booty hole, and I wanted to die.

"Come on, let's go to the water and try to soak it out." Flipping over, I crawled on my knees to the water and tried to open my pussy lips up as far as I could. Hoping I got it out, I stuck my finger inside and wanted to cry again.

"Nigga, this shit is turning to mud. Oh my God, what the fuck did you do to me?"

"Don't blame this shit on me. It ain't my fault you around here with dirty pussy." I looked at him and we both fell out laughing.

"Tico, help me. Stop laughing, this shit ain't funny. It hurts. Feel like ten niggas walking on my driveway kicking the rocks." He had tears in his eyes, and I was over his bullshit. I crawled all the way back to the room with him laughing hard walking behind me. When I made it to the bathroom, I ran some bath water and climbed in the tub. I should write every movie director or bitch that wrote sex on the beach as a love scene. Ain't shit sexy about that shit, and they got me fucked up.

Whoever named that drink after that shit couldn't have ever done it on a beach. Mufuckas was just saying what they thought sounded sexy because ain't no way. I climbed in the tub with my burning pussy praying this shit would eventually soak out. If not, I was gone be walking around with dessert pussy. There was no way I was taking my ass to a hospital telling them this shit.

Mantico St. Lauren

I don't know who looked more disappointed. Nadine or Dany, but they both had this dumb ass look on their faces. We were walking to our car about to head out for the airport, and they were trying to make me feel like shit. I had allowed Dany to keep me here for a week, but it was time to get back to business. I had shit to handle and money to collect. I could always bring her back and I told her that shit. No matter what I said, she was still walking around pouting.

"Make sure you call me. We can plan for you to come back soon." They hugged and me and Julio dapped it up.

"Aight, let's go." They hugged one more time as we climbed in the car. I closed my eyes because I didn't want to sit there watching her ass throw a tantrum the entire ride.

"Thank you for this Mantico. This was the best week of my life. I know I seem ungrateful, but I've never experienced anything like this before." Opening my eyes, I looked at her and she seemed so at peace. I know she thought I was just being an ass for no reason, but I had my reasons for wanting us to go back home.

"I may have a lead on who killed Kema. That's why we gotta go. I wasn't just trying to rain on your parade and shit. I love seeing you happy and we gone have time for all this shit. I promise you, anywhere you want to go, you got that. But, when it's time for me to handle my business, I need you to be okay with that too." Leaning over, she kissed me.

"Do you really think you know who it is?"

"Miesha showed up at one of the traps asking about you. Kept saying she needed to find you. Mink happened to be doing a pick up over there and overheard it. He got to questioning her on what she wanted with you, and she said she needed to find you, or she won't get paid. Miesha was at the shop when I came and got you. I don't believe in coincidences." I could tell she had a lot of thoughts running through her mind. I didn't want to get her hopes up, but I believed in my gut that Miesha had something to do with it.

"Oh my God. I thought she was trying to say her parents. Kema kept saying Mie, but I thought she was saying something else. It was her." I could see her getting worked up, but I wasn't allowing her to get involved in this.

"I got this. I promised you the head of whoever did this shit and I'm going to give you that. The only reason I told you any of this was to ease your mind about why we were leaving. I got you and I need you to know I will always have you."

"You better make that bitch suffer or we are done." She turned to look out the window and I nodded. Even though she couldn't see me, I heard her loud and clear. If Lil Mama wanted that bitch to suffer, that's exactly what the fuck I was going to do.

****

Walking into the warehouse, I had murder on my mind. Even though Miesha was going to meet her fate today, I needed her to tell me who the fuck is after Dany. She said if she didn't find her, she wouldn't get paid which tells me it's someone else behind this shit. I walked in the backroom and almost laughed. Mink was standing in front of Miesha pissing on her. Opening my bag, I pulled out a knife and walked over to her.

"I think when I told you I don't kill women and kids, you thought that shit pertained to you. See, you're not a woman. You're a low life, waste of fucking space. If you want to keep living in my fucking space, you need to tell me who the fuck is after Dany." She smiled and her empty mouth almost made me throw up.

"How is Dany doing? I need to find her." Taking the knife, I stabbed her in the top of her shoulder. She screamed out, but I didn't give a fuck.

"Who the fuck wants you to find Dany? It's my last time asking you."

"I don't know. A man walked up and told me he would pay me if I found her." Thinking of a different tactic, I pulled out some money from my pocket.

"Whatever he said he was giving you, I'll double it. That's only if you tell me though. If you don't, I'm going to drive this knife through your fucking head. Your choice."

"I don't remember his name, but he said you knew his brother and you killed him at a party." Thinking back to my birthday, I remembered Dany was dancing on a nigga. This was the second time Fil brought some niggas around me that was flaw. I looked at Mink and he grabbed his phone. Once I heard him tell Fil he was coming to grab him, I turned my attention back to Miesha.

"You deserve to die in the most gruesome way possible, but you are already a dead bitch walking. From the first moment I've met you, I knew you were a fucking low life. A useless bitch that got off on hurting kids. Even though yo life don't mean shit, I promised somebody special to me that you wouldn't breathe another day around this bitch." Grabbing the knife out her shoulder, I stabbed her in the eye. She was still screaming, and Mink ass was looking like he was about to throw up.

"Hurry up and kill this bitch."

"Go to the back and get some gasoline." Mink walked off shaking his head and I stared at Miesha as she screamed. I had no sympathy for her ass, and even though she was the first woman I've ever killed, she wasn't going to be the last. Knowing I needed to put an end to all this shit, I snatched the knife out her eye and stabbed her right in the temple of her head. Mink walked back in with the can of gas and was about to start pouring.

"Not yet. I'm about to bring her some company. You know what to do with the Fil situation." He nodded and I walked out to my car. Driving fast, I had one thing on my mind. It was too many mufuckas trying me right now and I was about to deaden all that shit. Pulling up, I grabbed my gun and got out of the car. I didn't wait on her to answer the door, I drew my leg back and kicked that bitch in. Celeste was walking past and screamed as I startled her.

"Oh my God, Tico. What are you doing here?" Not bothering to answer her, I hit her over the head with the butt of my gun. Her body immediately dropped, and I scooped the bitch up and carried her to my car. The bitch was doing too much, and I told her what was going to happen if she kept playing in my fucking face. This bitch played me from the jump and now she was about to see who the fuck I was.

It didn't take me long to get back to the warehouse. Grabbing the bitch by her hair, I dragged her ass toward the door. Celeste woke back up and began kicking and screaming. I continued to drag her until we were in the backroom with Miesha. When she saw her sitting there with a knife in her head, Celeste stopped fighting.

"Tico, I'm sorry. I know I have been acting up, but it was only because I was intimidated by that fat bitch. You changed when she came around and I was only trying to get your attention."

"So, when you brought yo dumb ass to my warehouse shooting in the air, was that for attention? Or, when you came back and shot at me. What was that for? Bitch, you been lying this entire time about Julio, and you think I'm about to allow you to walk my fucking streets?" When I thought about the camera footage I had, I waited until Dany went to sleep and looked at it. I didn't know what I was going to find, so I waited to watch it alone. This goofy bitch pulled a gun out and shot in the air. Then fell her dumb ass to the ground. I couldn't deal with this type of stupidity.

"I'm so sorry. I promise, I won't do it again." I know you won't." Raising my gun, I pulled the trigger causing her head to snap back.

"Hey nigga, you on a roll today huh. Fil and them are here." I nodded and I turned to see Fil and this goofy ass nigga that was at the club that night looking at me like he was tough.

"Tico, you know I ain't have shit to do with this. My cousins wanted to come party with you, so I let them. I warned them before they got there, so this on these niggas." The goofy nigga turned and looked at Fil shocked.

"You choosing this nigga over your blood? We are family and you choosing to kiss this nigga's ass instead of riding for yo people. Fuck you."

"Naw nigga, fuck you. Now, you wanna talk about family. Where the fuck were yall when I was out there starving? I had nowhere to go, but guess who took me the fuck in? This nigga. He fed me when I didn't have shit. I warned you niggas what would happen if you got out of pocket." I wasn't expecting it, but this nigga snatched a gun out of his waist and pulled the trigger. Fil's cousin fell to the ground and Fil turned to look at me.

"I know you don't trust me right now, but I'm loyal. Don't question that shit no more. If there is a problem, just tell me to handle it and I got you. I'm sorry about all this. Mink, I know I could never change what happened to Kema, and for that my nigga I will always live with that guilt. He told me he was the one that shot her when she wouldn't tell them where Dany was." He stood there awaiting his fate, so I put my gun in my waist.

"We good, but Fil. Don't bring no more new niggas around me. I can't speak for Mink, but we good." He looked towards Mink, and he remained silent for a while.

"We good. She at peace and we finally sent her the right company."

"Now that you niggas done sucking each other's dick, I need yall to find a new location. This bitch is done." Walking over to the gas can, I grabbed it and began pouring it over the bodies. Heading out to the other rooms, I poured it over the rest of the warehouse. "Mink, light this bitch up like Christmas morning." Nodding his head, he struck his lighter and we got the fuck out of dodge. From this day forward, I wasn't giving anymore second chances. Shit like this couldn't happen again. Next time, it could be Dany and I couldn't have that. Smiling, I couldn't wait to tell my Lil Mama she could rest easy now.

Danyelle Blakely

I couldn't sit around the house waiting to see what happened, so I took an Uber to Yvette's house. My nerves were shot, and I needed to be around someone. I got out of the car and walked to the door. I rang the bell and stood there nervously. When it opened, Yvette gave me a sympathetic look and grabbed me inside. From her expression, I'm assuming she thought I got into it with Tico. It was that it's going to be okay, yall just need some space look.

"Oh baby, what happened? Where is Tico?" I'm sure her ass was trying to figure out if I was there to kidnap her again.

"We're fine Yvette. He's out handling business and I didn't want to be at the house by myself." We walked into her tearoom and took a seat.

"I've been where you are. You have to decide if you're strong enough to deal with that lifestyle or get the fuck out of dodge. Me, I got the fuck on. I couldn't take it. For years, I wondered if I had done the right thing, but I know I did. I tried my best to save my child from the streets. His ass was just determined to be in them anyway. I was lucky. Manny knew what he lost, so he came back to me, but he waited until he was right for me." It took everything in me not to laugh. I wanted to tell her she had this shit all wrong, but she felt she was dropping knowledge. Me and her were not the same. I know people will never understand, but I wasn't built like that. I've always known what Tico did for a living, so that shit didn't bother me.

"I hear you Yvette. It's good that you got yo man though. You two seem so happy. I want that kind of love with your son." She nodded and I wondered what was going through her mind.

"Oh, I see. You're not stressed out about what he does. I'm just rambling and you looking at me like I'm crazy. I know most women could never do what I did, but I was trying to save my child. I love him and I would do anything to make sure he's okay." I interrupted her because she acted as if me staying made me less than her.

"I love him too and I choose to protect him. I'm not faulting what you did. A mother's love is like no other. You did what you felt was best. Me taking that charge for him, was me doing the same. From the moment I looked at your son, I knew he was going to be somebody. I know people say I'm dumb for what I did, but he was worth it." Her ass started smiling causing me to do it with her.

"I hope he is smart enough to know you're a keeper. That Celeste was never my taste." I giggled and rolled my eyes.

"She's finally out of the picture. You don't have to worry about that anymore. She knows I'm in his life now."

"If you will excuse me, I have to go and ask Manny did he talk to his son today. You know how men are." She damn near fell she jumped up so fast. I laughed and she looked at me crazy. "What's funny?"

"Everything with Julio is fine. Celeste was lying. So, as I said. She is out of our lives." Yvette sat down and smiled at me.

"You're a smart one Dany. Yeah, my son better marry your ass." As if he heard his name, he came bursting in the room out of breath and shit as if something was wrong.

"Why the fuck you didn't tell me you were leaving the house?"

"Umm, because I didn't know I had to. Is everything okay?" Yvette stood up and gave Tico a hug.

"I'll let you two talk. It's good to see you son. Come see me before you all leave." As soon as she was out of earshot, he went off again.

"Why the fuck are you just leaving out like that?"

"Nigga, what's the problem? I wanted some air, and you were gone. I couldn't sit around waiting on you to bring me some news."

"I thought you left me." I finally realized how scared he looked, and my heart softened.

"And leave that good dick for the next bitch, I would never. Why would you think that?"

"You said if I didn't make her suffer, you were done. I came back and you were gone. Maybe you thought a nigga couldn't do the shit."

"Footprints in the sand. I knew you would handle it. I just didn't want to sit around waiting on you to come back. I had no idea how long it was going to take, so I left. I'm sorry, and next time I'll call." Grabbing me, he pulled me in and kissed me hard.

"You fucking right. I handled everything, so we good."

"Was it Miesha?"

"In a way. She was trying to get to you. The guy I killed in the club wanted revenge, so he wanted you. Kema wouldn't give you up, so he killed her. Miesha was trying to lure you there." I couldn't believe that bitch.

"Thank you. My Best can rest easy now. My parents will take care of her. Take me home. Oh, and you can get rid of the condo." He looked at me and laughed.

"I called them a week ago and put that bitch on the market. If you had tried to leave you was gone be homeless as fuck." Shaking my head at him, I stared at him in disbelief.

"Nigga, don't play with me. I got all your credit cards and shit. I was gone be living in that deluxe apartment in the skyyyyy. I was gone use them bitches for everything."

"So, you was gone leave me?" Grabbing me by my ass, he scooped me up in the air as he bit my neck.

"No sir, I was not. Fuck, you think we can get a quicky in right here?"

"No the fuck you can't. Get yall nasty asses out my house. What grown ass niggas try to fuck at somebody else shit when they got they own house?" Embarrassed to hear Manny, I dropped my head and laughed.

"Dang, yall old asses hear everything. We ain't say shit when we walked in on yall fucking in the pool," Tico said, and I'm with him when he right.

"Yeah nigga, but we in our shit and yall showed up unannounced. Fuck you mean."

"You right. I got my own shit. I'll be to holla at you tomorrow to catch you up on everything. Right now, I'm in desperate need to feel my girl's insides." That was all he said before he carried me outside. When we got to his car, he took me to the driver side, so I was confused. Placing me on the ground, he opened the car door and slid the seat back.

"Mantico, what are you doing? I'm not about to fuck you in your parent's driveway." Shaking his head, he climbed inside.

"Naw, my girl can't be riding in Ubers and shit when I own ten damn vehicles. I'm about to teach you how to drive. This yo first lesson. Climb in on top of me." Nervous, I climbed inside and sat on his lap. He instructed me on how to adjust the mirrors and told me what each thing was. He even explained the gears. I guess he said I wasn't about to go in reverse in his shit. Finally, I was ready to go. I did everything he said and for the first few blocks, he kept his hands on top of mine as I drove. His touch was so soft and delicate. Finally, he let go and I continued to drive home. It wasn't long since his parents didn't live far from us, but I understood more now and couldn't wait for my next lesson. When I knew we were on our block, I started grinding my ass into his lap. I could feel his dick getting hard, and I was ready to be home. I needed to feel him inside of me. As soon as I parked, he grabbed me by my hair and pulled me in for a kiss.

"I love you Lil Mama." It was the first time he ever spoke those words and tears filled my eyes. I've loved this man for years and I thought someone like him could never love me back. I remember Kema thinking I was crazy, but I could hear her now up there screaming "Yesssssss Best. You did that shit. Give that nigga some pussy." Wiping the tears that fell from my eyes, I laughed hard as hell.

"Best, I'm about to fuck this nigga's brains loose." When I said that, Tico looked at me and then nodded in understanding. "I love you too, but I will love you more if you go get me some food. I'll be waiting on you naked."

"Say less." Climbing out of the car, I bent over and kissed him softly on his lips.

"For that shit, I think I'm going to try and give you some fye head tonight." His eyes got big and damn near fell out of his head.

"I'm straight on that. I'll be back Lil Mama." Laughing, I walked off into the house. I knew everything was going to be alright now. Looking up, I smiled. I knew my parents and Kema was smiling down on me. I been through hell and back, but I made it through. That day at the courts when I took that gun, I had no idea I would end up here. What was the lowest point in my life, turned out to be the best thing that ever happened to me. I couldn't tell anyone else how to write their story, but mine was written perfectly.

EPILOGUE...

"Why the fuck you keep hanging up the phone and shit every time I come in the room? I swear I will kill you dead if you fucking around on me. Don't play in my face, and I won't rearrange yours." Dany was going off, but I was used to it by now. Her hormones were all over the place, but it was sexy as fuck to me. Lil Mama was eight months pregnant, and I knew all that shit came with the territory. One minute she was hungry, the next she was crying, and then going the fuck off.

"I hung up the phone because I was done talking. You know ain't no bitch holding a candle to yo thick ass. Come here." She walked over to me as if she was waddling pouting the whole way. Laughing, I grabbed her to my lap and sat her down.

"I'm not thick anymore. I'm just big boned at this point. The baby done stretched me every way, but thin. You're not going to want me anymore." Shaking my head, I used my fingers to wipe her tears away.

"Dany, you ain't gained nothing but stomach, but I wouldn't care if you did. It's not a scar, a stretch mark, or a pound you could get that would make me change how I feel about you. I'm a grown ass nigga and I know what the fuck happens when you carry a child. Every curve on yo body belongs to me, don't ever forget that shit. I know you emotional because of the pregnancy, but I'm not with that insecure shit. You have no reason to be. Now, ride this dick so we can go out to dinner. I'm hungry." Just like that, her mood had changed. Smiling, she pulled her shirt up and I slid my dick out of my pants.

When I felt her go down on my shit, I almost said fuck what we had going on tonight. I wouldn't mind laying up with Lil Mama all night, but it was some shit I had to do. Her ass started going crazy and that big ass was bouncing like a mufucka on my dick. I slapped her ass cheeks getting ready to take off when she started screaming and moaning like crazy.

"Fuck Mantico, I'm about to cum." Before I could pick up the pace and try to force mine out, Dany started shaking.

Leaning down, she kissed me and stood up. Pregnancy had her acting like a nigga, and I felt like a bitch. She could have at least let a nigga precum. "Okay, I'm going to wash my ass, be ready." Shaking my head, I removed my clothes and stood up.

"I'm going to the other shower. I bought you something to wear tonight, it's on the bed." Walking to the other bathroom, I climbed inside and washed my ass. When I was done, I grabbed a towel and got dressed. For the first time in my life, I threw on some casual clothes. Instead of the jackets I normally wear, I threw on a blazer over my t shirt. Grabbing my Tom Ford casual boots, I put them on, and I was ready. Dany came walking out looking sexy as fuck and I was tempted to go bend her ass over, but I knew everyone was waiting on us.

"Well don't you look dapper. This is a nice look on you Mantico." Grabbing her around the waist, I led her downstairs to the car. It took us ten minutes to get to our location, but this nigga was over there mouth open snoring and slobbing.

Shaking my head, I tapped her letting her know we arrived. "Oh, this what we doing now? You beat women? You're a fucking woman beater Tico?" Shaking my head, I laughed at the bullshit she was spitting.

"Naw, we here Lil Mama. Wake yo ass up and wipe yo mouth." Embarrassed, she grabbed a napkin and cleaned her face. Getting out, I walked over to her side and let her out. As soon as I grabbed her hand, she snatched it away and started screaming. Panic came over me as I turned to see what was wrong.

"Oh my God, Tico. What is this?" I followed her eyes and realized she noticed the sign.

"A taste of Kema's. I bought you a restaurant. I'm sure you don't want to sit around the house all day doing nothing, so instead of having you getting into dumb shit, I got you something I thought you would love. Since yo ass always eating, I figured food would be your passion. Come on, let's go look inside." She was crying, but this time I knew they were happy tears. We walked inside and she was surprised to find everyone there. My parents, the crew, even Nadine and Julio flew in. Her ass cried as she thanked everyone for coming as she walked around oohing and ahhing at all the décor.

"This is the best gift ever. I love it Mantico." Manny walked up and handed me a box, as I nodded towards this guy in the back. He walked over to Dany.

"Excuse me miss. I was your uncle's attorney and I stopped by to give you this paperwork. You are the only survivor, so all of his money and estates go to you." He passed her the envelope as she turned to me for understanding. I winked at her, and she smiled. When she told me her uncle played her, I found his ass wanting to talk to him about rekindling with Dany, so she could have family. They ass was out there living the good life knowing she had no one, so I killed him and his bitch ass wife.

"Thank you sir. I'll come by your office or call you tomorrow to talk about the rest." I nodded to Yvette, so she distracted her as I nodded to the DJ, he began to play Bonnie and Clyde. She finally turned to me, and I was down on one knee nervous as fuck.

"Danyelle, from the moment I met yo ass you were a pain. You were always trying to make sure a nigga was straight, but yo young ass wasn't even good. I thought Lil Mama gotta be crazy looking out for me when she can't even look out for herself. It wasn't until you went away that I realized I had a rare find. You cared about what happened to me before I cared myself and you never stopped. You held me down no matter what and I will always be grateful to you for that. You're my peace and I won't be good until you're carrying my name. So, Lil Mama will you and baby Tico marry me?" She got on her knees and hugged me.

"I will always hold you down. Yes, I will marry you." She cried and a nigga had to fight back my emotions as I placed the ring on her finger.

"Danyelle St. Lauren. That shit sound sexy as fuck."

"Footprints." Mink walked up holding a pic of Kema as he congratulated us.

"Why you got this big ass pic of Best?" Mink shrugged and laughed.

"Shid, Best said she wanted to come too. She wasn't missing this shit for nothing in the world. Fuck you thought this was. Her words not mine." We all laughed as we went to mingle with the guests. It was a few times I could see her getting emotional, but every time she looked at me, she got it together and start smiling again. That was all I ever wanted. Was to be to her what she was to me. Peace.

THE END...

KEEP UP WITH LATOYA NICOLE

Like my author page on fb @misslatoyanicole

My fb page Latoya Nicole Williams

IG AuthorLatoyaNicole

Twitter Latoyanicole35

Snap Chat iamTOYS

Reading group: Toy's House of Books

Email latoyanicole@yahoo.com

☐

OTHER BOOKS BY LATOYA NICOLE (AVAILABLE ON

AMAZON)

NO WAY OUT: MEMOIRS OF A HUSTLA'S GIRL 1-2

GANGSTA'S PARADISE 1-2

ADDICTED TO HIS PAIN (STANDALONE)

LOVE AND WAR: A HOOVER GANG AFFAIR 1-4

CREEPING WITH THE ENEMY: A SAVAGE STOLE

MY HEART PART 1-2

I GOTTA BE THE ONE YOU LOVE (STANDALONE)

THE RISE AND FALL OF A CRIME GOD: PHANTOM

AND ZARIA'S STORY 1-2

ON THE 12TH DAY OF CHRISTMAS MY SAVAGE

GAVE TO ME

A CRAZY KIND OF LOVE: PHANTOM AND ZARIA

14 REASONS TO LOVE YOU: A LATOYA NICOLE

ANTHOLOGY

SHADOW OF A GANGSTA

THAT GUTTA LOVE 1-2

LOCKED DOWN BY HOOD LOVE 1-2

THE BEARD GANG CHRONICLES 2 (THE TEASE)

THROUGH THE FIRE: A STANDALONE NOVEL

DAUGHTER OF A HOOD LEGEND 1-2

CRAVING THE LOVE OF A THUG 1-2

SON OF A CRIME GOD, DAUGHTER OF A HOOVER 1-3

A RUTHLESS KIND OF LOVE 1-3

SAVAGE OF THE NIGHT: URBAN PARANORMAL

SON OF A CRIME GOD, DAUGHTER OF A HOOVER THE WEDDING

MADE TO LOVE YOU 1-2: NOVELLA

CHOSEN BY A STREET KING 1-3: COLLAB WITH K. RENEE

CHECKMATE 1-2

LOVED BY A BEAST: A HALLOWEEN SHORT

NEVER KNEW A THUG LIKE THIS (STANDALONE)

FOREVER MY THUG 1-2 COLLAB WITH K RENEE

A PRINCESS AND HER HITTA (STANDALONE)

LOVE IN THE CARTEL 1-2

FALLING FOR THE PLUG'S DAUGHTER 1-2

BLINDED BY HOOD LOVE 1-3 COLLAB WITH A.J DAVIDSON

TIS THE SEASON TO MEND A HITTA'S HEART

RIDING FOR THAT THUG LOVE PART 1-2

COMING TO THE HOOD NOVELLA

CHRISTMAS WITH A BILLIONAIRE

A HOOVER GANG CHRISTMAS

Made in United States
Troutdale, OR
08/19/2024

22159993R00189